Zaddy Issues

By Maceo Reed

Zaddy Issues

Zaddy Issues

Antioch, TN 37013

ISBN 979-8-218-10545-7

Published by Maceo Keed, Antioch, TN 37013

Printed in the U.S.A.

William "Deek" Harris, December 2022

Cover designed by Thomas Adams

Zaddy Issues

Zaddy Issues

Contents

Zaddy Issues

Zaddy Issues

Chapter 1

The Single Life

Saturday nights used to mean that it was time to hit the club scene with the girls to get their drink on. Ebonee and her girls' Gina and Nicole were the talk of the night whenever they walked inside of any spot. You would be hard pressed to find three chicks hotter than them in Charlotte, NC. But now that everyone seemed to be "booed up" except for Ebonee, she doesn't get out as much. Not only Saturday nights but most nights she found herself curled up on the couch watching television or reading some erotic book by her favorite author Deek Harris. The saddest thing was that if it wasn't for his books and her little toys, her lady parts would get zero action. She had convinced herself for months that she didn't need a man. Her girls tried hooking her up with men but none of the fellows they brought to her had the total package. Either they were cute but thuggish, well off but too arrogant, well built but poor hygiene and the list went on. None of them were worth the time or the energy to her. The last guy that she had was the man of her dreams until she realized that he wasn't a dream but a nightmare instead. Darrius was fresh out of auto mechanic school and appeared to have a promising future ahead of him. Despite the fact that he was ten years younger than Ebonee and working at a garage as a mechanic, she found it ambitious. Her girlfriends teased and called her a "cougar" for robbing the cradle. In her defense, Ebonee would argue that thirty-four was not old enough to be considered a "cougar" yet. Her follow up argument was that he laid pipe better than any other man that she had been with. That only brought on more ridicule for "dick whipped" jokes. She took it like a champ and overlooked them and as well as most of Darrius' youthfulness. But what she couldn't overlook was him receiving titty pics at three o'clock in the morning from a number saved as "Pizza Hut" on the cell phone that she provided for him. Come to find out, he was playing more than "Call of Duty" on the Xbox. He was playing "Call Some Booty" in three or four female boxes. He was a master manipulator and that forced her to put a wall of steel around herself.

For months Ebonee wallowed in pity and self doubt. Regardless to anything her friends said she felt as though it was something about herself that turned Darrius to those other females. Like a lot of southern women, Ebonee was thicker than cold molasses. She was blessed with more curves than a racetrack, but her insecurities led her to believe that it was something about herself that pushed Darrius to those younger and slimmer girls. She was fully aware of the extra pounds she gained after she stopped going out dancing as often. But she thought that he liked her full figure. At least that's what he told her anyway. She was in a rut for quite a while behind Darrius. Her girls had almost given up on her until her closest friend Gina introduced her to the wonderful world of erotic tales from her collection of books. Her initial introduction was a Christmas gift from Gina. It was a holiday book of erotic tales called "Dear Santa... I Can Explain". It was just what she needed at the time. It had been months since she had the pleasures of feeling a man inside of her. The book went well with a glass of wine and her favorite vibrator. Although it couldn't provide the same satisfaction of feeling the touch of her man holding her body or smacking her ass, it still provided some much-needed climatic relief. She enjoyed it so much that she found herself seeking out more erotic novels to help curb her increasingly salacious appetite for intimacy. She eventually began to believe that she didn't need a man as her adult toy collection grew as rapidly as her desires grew. It eventually became a time-consuming addiction that had little to no boundaries. She would masturbate two to three times a day sometimes if the urge was really bad. There were times that it was so bad that she was presenting potentially self-destructive challenges to herself. It was when she accepted her own challenge to make herself cum in her office before a meeting that she realized she needed some real dick. Toys and books were fun, but she knew that she couldn't continue down the "slippery when wet" road that she was on. She needed to feel the pulsation of a man. She longed for the feeling of a man's heavy breathing on the back of her neck while getting fucked hard from behind. There was no toy that she could buy that would grunt out the words "take this dick!" She missed how long and hard Darrius would get inside of her. It was time to get back on the dating scene she figured.

Ebonee knew that if she called Gina that she would definitely be onboard for helping her find a man. After all, it was her little naughty gift that ignited her urges. So, who better to pick for this new adventure to find a new "Mr. Man?" The weekend was only a couple of days away, so she invited Gina over to her place to have some wine and to put together a master game plan for her mission. Gina had been proposed to by five different men before she found Kareem, the love of her life. With five years of marriage in, the two of them exhibited the type of true love that Ebonee was seeking. Hell, it was the kind of love everyone sought. After Darrius, Ebonee just didn't trust her own judgments. She felt

Zaddy Issues

the need to call in the big guns for reinforcements if she was going to do it right this time. So, she was willing to trust the fate of her love life in the hands of her bestie. When Saturday night came Ebonee heard a knock at the door. "Who is it" she asked as she trotted to the front door. "Child if you don't open this door…" the voice on the other side responded. When she opened the door, she found not only Gina standing in front of her, but Nicole was right by her side. "Oh my God! Nicole, I didn't know you were coming too. I would have bought more wine. I figured you might've had to help open the club with Spade tonight. That's why I didn't even bother to call you." Ebonee confessed. "Bitch PLEASE! That's my last name on that club. Anthony knows that when the "Bitch" signal shines in the sky like Batman's, I drop everythang! Ok?" Nicole exclaimed with emphasis as they walked through the door. Ebonee closed the door and issued her proverbial three snaps in the air and said "ok Mrs. Spade! Do yo thang then!" She followed Gina and Nicole into her living room and took a seat while they hung their coats in the closet. "Well, we're going to have to make a run to the store eventually I only grabbed two bottles of wine." Ebonee explained as Nicole and Gina took their seats. "Wine? Girl stops!" Nicole demanded. She reached inside of her purse and pulled out an unopened bottle of Casamigos. "Damn some wine. We need the heavy shit tonight honey" Nicole said. Then Gina reached inside of her bag and added, "And I brought the margarita mix. So, bring me your laptop and take these two bottles and get in the kitchen whipping up some of your fire ass margaritas because we're here all night tonight babe." Ebonee jumped to her feet with a smile and said, "say less chica."

Chapter 2

Operation Mr. Man

The three of them sat up all night drinking Ebonee's notoriously heavy poured margaritas and taking shots of tequila. They managed to narrow down a list of all of the things that Ebonee wanted in a man and relationship. Then they ran down a list of all of the men that they knew in the city in hopes of coming up with at least one potential candidate. The biggest problem was that most of the men that they knew were either dogs, in a relationship already or someone that they'd known long enough to know that if there was anything there that it would have happened already. But knowing that Charlotte was a pretty big city, there had to be more men out there that they didn't already know. The club scene was definitely out of the question. The last thing they wanted to do was find another player. Eventually Gina proposed the bright idea of trying a dating website. Initially Ebonee was s bit reluctant of the idea. "I don't know about this. I've always kind of looked at those types of sites as being for 'thirsty' folks." Without hesitation Nicole glared at Ebonee and said "bitch you are thirsty! You're around here playing with these damn vibrating toys so much yo teeth be chattering like you're freezing when you talk sometimes. Stop it! We're getting you some real dick by any means necessary. I'm like Malcolm X round this piece." Nicole was what they considered the OG with a heart of gold of their little crew. But don't let her good looks full you. She grew up in the streets of Atlanta and knew how to handle herself if the situation called for it. The two of them had witnessed multiple times when Nicole went from zero to bitch mode in lightning speed. But as long as you stayed on her good side then she was on your side. She could be a little slick at the mouth at times but that was cool with them. They knew she never meant any harm. She was only two years older than Ebonee and Gina, but her life experiences far outweighed those of Ebonee or Gina's. Ebonee of course folded to Nicole's colorful realization of her journey to find Mr. Man and allowed them to create an account on "Black and Single Charlotte."

Ebonee's views on finding a man were more along the old fashion traditions. She believed in the idea of being courted and love at first sight. She was a hopeless romantic with a lustful appetite for men. Unlike Nicole, Ebonee grew up in a lot more structured home as a child. Her father was a preacher at a mega church in Greensboro, NC. The closest she got to the streets was watching videos on Rap City. Her

Zaddy Issues

parents were overly protective of her as a child. But when she went off to college there was no one there to hide her behavior from. She explored every kind of adventure that crossed her mind. She got drunk for the first time, drove a car for the first time, went to school games, hung out until daybreak and plenty of other things that most teens had done at least once before going off to college. None of those things could match losing her virginity to a slick talking upper classman named Charles Banks. He taught her things in bed that would make a porn star blush. She may have been valedictorian of her graduating class in high school, but she was also an honor student in the bedroom in college. As a young adult her sexual desires spiked tremendously. Her sex drive skyrocketed to the point that she occasionally would enjoy threesomes. More often than not, they would include another female rather than a man. Her twenties were full of sexual explorations that most could only dream about. That was one of the many benefits acquired from being pretty with a body that looked handcrafted. But even goddesses like Ebonee want to settle down eventually, even if it means finding "Mr. Man" on a dating site.

After staying up all night drinking and binge-watching movies on Hulu, the three of them woke up in Ebonee's living room the next morning. A repeating high pitched

Zaddy Issues

pinging sound coming from Ebonee's laptop worked just as effectively as any alarm clock. Gina was the first of the three to get to her feet to investigate. Halfway asleep still Gina staggered over to the chiming computer still opened on the countertop. "GIRL...YOUR ASS IS POPPING ON HERE!" Gina screamed. "Come look at how many likes and comments you have on these pictures already. What the hell? Where was this shit when I was single?" she continued. Ebonee and Nicole rushed over to see just what Gina was raving about. "Damn! I didn't even know there were that many single men in Charlotte" Gina added. "Yeah, that's definitely a lot of men. But how many of them do you really think are truly single? Think about it. Some men will do anything for some pussy. Your job now is to narrow it down and try to figure out who's real and who's not" Nicole wisely suggested. "How am I supposed to do that? There're a hundred and eighteen friend requests. I can't talk to a hundred and eighteen men" Ebonee questioned. "For you to be so pretty and smart, you sure are dumb" Nicole expressed with a look of genuine concern. "You don't have to go out with them silly. You look through the profile pictures for crazy shit. But you're on your own with that. I'm about to take my ass home" Nicole boldly said while heading to get her coat. Gina burst out laughing then followed Nicole to the

Zaddy Issues

closet saying "yeah sis, I'm heading home too. I'll give you a call a little later. But get some sleep and check it later because you're probably going to be having men hitting you up all morning. Let the wave die down and check it after you wake up. But I told you last night, that picture in the swimsuit with all that ass out was going to get them." The three of them had a good laugh at Gina as they headed to the door.

Chapter 3

Why Not

Ebonee spent the majority of her day and night sifting through her increased list of callers. By six o'clock that evening she had narrowed down the one hundred and thirty-eight number of men to a modest ten. Those ten men looked to be more aligned with what she was looking for in a man. She was unsure on how to approach them without appearing to be thirsty or an easy lay. She clicked the heart buttons on their profiles to notify them that she liked their profiles." This is stupid" she said to herself standing in her kitchen staring at the laptop on the counter. She slammed the laptop and began to prepare her dinner for the evening. If there was anything that she loved more than sex it had to be cooking and crafting. Just as she was placing her homemade meatloaf in the oven her phone rang. "Hey girl. What you up to?" she asked answering the phone with a giggle. It was Gina. "Oh, nothing much. I just woke up a couple of hours ago. Girl I was BEAT! You were a little extra heavy handed on those margaritas last night" Gina responded. "Yeah, but they were good as hell though, won't they?" Ebonee replied. "Now I can't argue with you there. You make better margaritas than most of these restaurants around here. But anyway, I called to see what's going on with the site. There were some fine ass men on there. Any luck yet?" Gina asked. "Oh yeah! There's a lot of fine ass men on there alright. But like ya'll said, 'I had to pick through some'. And trust me there were a lot of suspect ass dudes too. Some of them were just oozing with drama and headache even through their pictures. But my favorite ones are the ones that feel the need to put his salary in his bio. Like, sit your ass down somewhere before a bitch come through and take all of your money. But I did manage to put together a choice of ten brothers that I found interesting. I clicked the heart on their profiles then instantly felt crazy." Ebonee expressed. "Ok...ok. That's a start. It's not crazy though. Plenty of people have actually had some success on online dating sites. My cousin Cheryl in Chicago found her husband on a site just like this one. You just have to give it a chance. You never know" Gina suggested. "I know but what if I run into another Darrius or worse" she questioned. "Then you throw his ass back to the streets and move on with your life. Mr. Man is out there somewhere. Times are different now. There's nothing wrong with a woman being the hunter these days. Men swear up and down that they want a woman that knows what she wants and willing to go get it. We've been

Zaddy Issues

friends ever since you moved to Charlotte, and you've always been a go getter. When you first came here you were determined to be the first black female to own a five-star restaurant in Uptown Charlotte. Now look at you. Girl you are a rare find. You don't have to settle for any ole man. But you will have to put forth some effort in order to find the right man. He's out there! You'll get him just like you got your restaurant." Gina sincerely advised.

Later that night after a hot shower Ebonee found comfort air drying wrapped in her favorite robe. She took a seat a plush wingback chair that sat in the adjacent corner from her bed. It was one of her favorite places to be ever. Sitting there with her feet curled up under her with a good book and a glass of wine always put her in her happy place. That night instead of her usual ritual she switched from reading a book to grabbing her laptop. During her shower she thought about all of the things she and Gina discussed. She figured that she might as well check to see if she'd had any responses. Six of her top ten choices had actually responded. All six of them were extremely pleasing to the eye. She didn't want to be bombarded with a bunch of messages, so she only responded back to the three most recently received messages. She responded to all of them with the same simple message. "I really like your pictures" it read. It was a way of opening the

Zaddy Issues

floor for discussion without being too aggressive she figured. Within a matter of seconds, the sound of a high-pitched bell sounded off from her laptop. It was an almost immediate response. Surprisingly it was from the best-looking guy out of all ten that she sent a message. "Thank you! I really like your pictures also. You have a beautiful smile" it read. Instantly she began to smile as if she was commanded to do so. It had been quite a while since she had been complimented by a man and it felt good. "Thank you. Are you originally from Charlotte?" she asked. "Yes, I was born and raised here. What about you" he answered. She gave him a brief run down on where she was from and how she landed in Charlotte after college, but she left out the fact that she was the owner of "Uptown Cuisine". That was as need to know information that she would share later if they continued to talk down the road. But for now, all he needed to know was that she moved there after college to pursue her dreams of becoming a master chef. In return he shared that he was a personal athletic trainer for several of the professional athletes in Charlotte. From the looks of his pictures Ebonee could easily see that he was in great shape. He wasn't the overly muscular type that couldn't put his arms down by his side. He was really well defined though and several shirtless pictures on his profile page provided

Zaddy Issues

plenty of visually pleasing proof. "I don't know that I could see myself calling you T-Dawg. What's your government name? If you don't mind me asking" Ebonee inquired. "Lol lol...T-Dawg is what I go by professionally. In my line of work no one wants to get trained by a guy named Trevor Wiseman. At least I would rather be trained by T-Dawg than Trevor. But I use it on here because I didn't want to put my government on here. Just like I'm sure your parents didn't name you 'realchik89'...lol" he cleverly countered. They continued chatting for another hour or so about likes, dislikes, the future and most other normal first conversational things.

Chapter 4

Going Out on A Limb

Ebonee and the girls met up for their every other Thursday lunch at her restaurant "Uptown Cuisine" to catch up on what was going on in each other's lives. The weather was being extra cooperative considering early fall afternoons in the Carolinas can be a bit deceiving sometimes. They choose to sit outside to soak in some of the much-appreciated warmth rather than sitting at their usual table inside. "So, when are you and your new boo going to meet up" Gina asked before taking a bite of her food. Ebonee blushed and said "Well actually he asked to take me out this Saturday" "Ok...ok! Where is he taking you" Nicole asked. "I don't know just yet. All I know is that he said to where something casual and comfortable" answered with a little giggle. "Look at you are glowing and shit like some little schoolgirl or something" Nicole joked. They all laughed for a moment. Then Ebonee extended both hands for Gina and Nicole to each grab one then said "I want to thank both of you for making me sign up for Black and Single Charlotte. I don't know where this journey may take me but what I do know is that I haven't felt this alive in a long time. And if you two hadn't been so committed to getting me out of my slump that I might not have met Trevor. I owe it all to you two. Now I'm not saying that he's the one for me, but he's given me a reason to feel sexy again and I like that shit." Ebonee released their hands then sat back in her seat and continued, "And it definitely helps that he is FIIIIINE AS HELL! He sent me a picture of him standing in front of a mirror after his shower wearing nothing but a white towel around his waist. Girl his dreadlocks were still wet and glistening and so was six pack and chest. But none of him was wetter than I was when I saw the bulge in that towel! Giiiiiirl…I got horny and nervous at the same time." A small roar of laughter erupted at the table causing others sitting at nearby tables to all turn their attentions to the ladies. Slightly embarrassed as if their conversation may have been loud enough for others to hear, they all hushed each other while giggling under their breaths.

After lunch Ebonee walked Gina and Nicole to their cars to say goodbye then headed back to the restaurant. As she approached the patio area of her restaurant, she noticed there was a cell phone sitting on the table they were sitting at. She rushed over to retrieve it because she knew that it had to be one of theirs. Just as she was checking to see whose phone it

Zaddy Issues

was, her waitress was about to seat a very well dressed older black man with a full salt and pepper beard at a table across from her. Ebonee had her fair share of experience in the fashion world while helping Gina get her boutique up and running. She attended countless fashion shows all across America as well as overseas. She'd also seen many of her fashionable patrons that were wealthy come in wearing some of the finest of clothes. But this man looked as if he had stepped straight off of a page in a GQ magazine. Everything about him screamed tailor-made from his suit to the fedora he was sporting. His well cultivated beard stood bold against his strong richly dark skin. A chill ran down her spine when she heard him say "thank you" to the waitress for showing him to his table. Slowly she turned to head inside but nearly stumbled over a chair because she couldn't take her eyes off of him. He jumped from his seat to rush to Ebonee's aide. Before he could get to her, she had regained her footing and held her hand up to politely decline saying "I'm ok but thanks." Embarrassed beyond measure she turned and walked off quickly to get back inside. She nearly ran over one of the servers on the way to her private bathroom in her office. Once she was inside of her office, she slammed the door behind her and leaned against to gather herself. She hadn't been that flustered since she met Tupac backstage at

Zaddy Issues

her college homecoming concert. She nearly fainted then and wasn't in much better shape at the time. By the time she made it to the bathroom she realized there was nothing that she could do with her panties other to take them off. There was no way that she could walk around for the rest of the day with panties as wet as those.

As she was finishing freshening up, her phone began to ring. It was Trevor. "Hey you! I was just talking about you" she answered. "Is that right? All good things I hope" he responded. The mere sound of his deep voice made her melt like ice cream in the sun. She giggled and said "of course. You haven't given me any reason to say anything otherwise." He chuckled then replied "cool. So, listen I know we have plans for Saturday night and all, but I was wondering if we could get together sooner. I was thinking maybe we could catch the Thursday night football game. The Panthers are playing the Rams and one of the guys that I train is on the team. He gets me great box seats. I'd love for you to join me. What do you say?" He knew from their many phone conversations that she was a huge football fan. "Is this a trick question" she asked laughing. "Of course! I'd love to go to the game with you rather sitting home alone watching the very game on my couch. Hell yes is what I say. The number one offense against the number two defense. Let's gooooo!" she emphatically answered. Trevor was excited about how excited Ebonee was. "Cool. The game starts at 8:20pm. How about I pick you up around five o'clock so that we can grab a drink or two to pregame a little before we get there? Or would you rather that we meet somewhere uptown and catch an Uber somewhere then go to the game?" Trevor suggested. As much as she was feeling their vibe Ebonee wasn't ready to give out her address just yet. "How about meeting me at my job? I work uptown at Uptown Cuisine's remember? It's only a couple of blocks away. You can park in the back where the owner parks. She's cool as hell and doesn't mind me parking back there. That way we can grab a bite to eat and a couple of drinks there. We can walk to the stadium and save that Uber money for more food and drinks at the game. What do YOU say?" Ebonee redirected. "I'd say I like your plan very much. However, there's just one little flaw in your plan" he said. "And what's that?" Ebonee questioned. She thought it was a pretty solid suggestion and struggled to find the flaw. "And what's the flaw?" she asked. Trevor laughed and said "the flaw is your job. Well to be more specific, I said that I train professional athletes. I'm not one. I would love to have a meal and drinks at Uptown Cuisine, but drinks alone would probably cost more than my week's salary. Then to throw in food too? Oh yeah, I'd have to rob a couple of my clients in an alley somewhere to be able to afford that" he jokingly explained. They both laughed and Ebonee knew that her prices were just as exclusive as the food. But when you have a world-renowned chef like Guillermo Guzman running your kitchen you can charge whatever you'd like. "Now you're exaggerating but I get it. Don't trip. I can take care of the bill at the UC. It's the least that I can do if you're getting us these great seats from your mystery client. I know people that hook me up to. And I'm not telling you who my people are either" she said in a childishly teasing voice. Trevor laughed at her childish mockery and said "Ok cool. What time should I be there?" She thought for a moment then said "be there around four o'clock. I'll clock out an hour early. Anytime after that the city starts to close the streets off and you'll catch hell trying to get to the restaurant."

After they finished their phone call Ebonee jumped straight into her daily work routine. She was about thirty minutes into checking over her inventory numbers when Candace her day shift manager came knocking at her office door. "Come in" she shouted at the door without looking up. "Ms. Lawrence there's a gentleman at the bar asking to speak with the manager. He's upset and complaining about his meal being overcooked. And you know how fired up Guillermo

Zaddy Issues

can get when someone insults his work. I tried talking to him but when Guillermo heard about the complaint he came from the back and went Chef Ramsey on the guy. Now the guy wants to speak with someone over me. Do you want me to call the police, or did you want to try to speak with him first?" Candace explained. Frustrated and in disbelief with all of that Ebonee held her head up and said with disgust, "no…no need to call the police unless he becomes violent. You can let him know that I'll be there in a moment. And make sure Guillermo stays in the back away from the knives." Candace nodded her head and closed the door behind her.

Ebonee sat back in her chair with her head held back her eyes closed and kept repeating to herself a popular internet chant "holy spirit activate…activate…activate! Holy spirit activate…activate…activate!" After a few of those she was ready to put on a fake smile long enough to deescalate what appeared to be a blown out of proportion. She walked to the door and took a deep breath then opened it. Immediately she could hear an argument brewing so loudly that other customers were turning around to see what was going on. It was not a good look for business. Ebonee trotted over to make Guillermo return to the kitchen while she addressed the irate man. But before she could open her mouth to get a word out the guy turned to Ebonee and said "no wonder this place is so poorly run. You have a wetback cooking and a coon that's running the whole operation." His words made everyone in the restaurant gasp at the same time. "EXCUSE ME?" Ebonee screamed. "I didn't stutter. You heard me damn it!" he barked back at Ebonee. She took a deep breath preparing to light into his ass both verbally and physically. She was stopped in her tracks when she heard deep rumbling voice coming up from behind her saying "she might have heard you, but I didn't. Say it again. Tell me what you said sir! I missed it. But I promise you I won't miss it this time." Ebonee whipped around to see who was speaking. Along with everyone else she was shocked to see that it was the older gentleman that was sitting in the patio area earlier. He walked up and stood directly behind Ebonee. Even in her heels the older man dwarfed her. He didn't appear to be as massive of a man when she saw him earlier. But then again, it wasn't very hard to seem gigantic when she only stood 5'6" in her 3" heels. The white guy was clearly out of sorts at that point but wanted to look tough. "You don't scare me! I know people you know" the white man bucked. The older black man opened his arms then smiled and said "you don't know anyone like me though. I can promise you that!" The white guy stood frozen but refused to back down. "You don't

Zaddy Issues

know. You have no idea who I know" he continued. The older black man gently nudged Ebonee to the side to step from behind her in order to move closer to the white guy. He never took his eyes off of the white guy while the white guy clearly was surveying the building for an emergency escape route. The older gentleman stood directly in front of Ebonee and continued "No I don't know who you know. But what I do know is they're obviously not here with you now. I also know that they can't get to you before you find yourself in imminent danger that you might not be able to get out of before they can get to you. Now I'm going to ask you again. Tell me what you told her." The white guy threw his napkin down on the floor and said, "this is ridiculous!" with a look of hatred. "No, you're ridiculous! Your behavior is ridiculous! Everything that you have done is ridiculous. And do you see that little girl at that table with her family? She's been recording this whole ridiculous fiasco the whole time" the gentleman added. Everyone looked over and sure enough there was a child holding her cell phone aimed directly at them all. "You know what else is ridiculous? The fact that you're probably trending online by now means that whatever line of work you're in is probably in jeopardy. No one is going to want to do business with the racist that went viral for showing his true colors. But what's going to be the most ridiculous thing of all is the ass whooping that I give you if you don't pick that napkin up off of the floor like you have some sense and apologize to everyone that you disrespected" the older black man said while smiling the entire time. Reluctantly the white guy bent over and picked up the napkin then slammed it on the table. He turned to walk away but was stopped when Guillermo jumped in front of him. "I believe you're forgetting the most important clause in our agreement. That's the only way you can leave out of here walking upright on your own. Otherwise, someone's going to have to carry you out of here" the black man said. The white guy turned back around to face the group and sheepishly muttered "I'm sorry. Can I go now?" Guillermo was quick to answer "YES! And don't ever come back!"

Everyone watched the man stomp out of the restaurant. An explosion of applause burst out as the door closed behind the man. Every customer the building was clapping for outstanding display of chivalry they had all just witnessed. Ebonee turned to her knight in shining armor and said, "I can't thank you enough for what you did just now." He just continued to smile as he had the whole time and said "don't mention it. Any real man would have done the same. Besides, your chef didn't need to get locked up and deprive the city of his works of art while sitting in a jail cell behind that clown. Plus, it's been a while since I've had that kind of rush. It was actually pretty fun." Ebonee began to blush, and her light skin instantly turned bright red. The way he stood up to that man made him even sexier to Ebonee. "Well Mr....I'm sorry. I don't know your name" Ebonee started out saying. "It's Malcolm. My name is Malcolm Cox. You can lose the Mr. Cox thing. Please...call me Malcolm" he requested. Again, she blushed even more. It was so obvious that Candace and Guillermo excused themselves and return to work so that they could talk alone. "Well Mr....excuse me...Malcolm we appreciate your kindness and assistance in handling the situation. And as a token of my appreciation not only as the owner but more so as a black woman I'd like to offer you a complimentary meal for two including a bottle of Ace Champaign or bottle of our best wine of your choice whenever you choose. I would love to meet the Mrs. as well" Ebonee expressed. Malcolm flashed his pearly white teeth and said "I just may take you up on that offer. However, dinner for one and a drink or two of bourbon will suffice Mrs...." The fact he addressed her as Mrs. let her know that he was trying to see if she was married just as she did. "It's Miss Lawrence. But you can call me Ebonee" she responded with a smile. "Ebonee...that's a beautiful name. It's definitely fitting for such a beautiful woman. But I would more than likely be dining alone. My wife passed away nearly ten years ago now." Malcolm answered. "Oh, I'm so sorry" Ebonee replied with shame. She placed her hand over her lips from embarrassment. Gently he pulled her hand away and said "Nooo it's fine. You're good." as embarrassed as she was, she was also a bit relieved to know that she wasn't lusting in her mind over someone's husband. Just the thought of her cheating with a married man had always been a huge turn off for her. But a widower was something different and new to her as well. She had never been with a man more than two or three years older than her let alone anyone that was old enough to be old enough to be a widower. "Well Mr....I mean Malcolm. I'm going to have Candace to make sure that you get one of my business cards for you to give me a call whenever you are ready to cash in on your meal or if there's ever anything that I can do for you. Enjoy the rest of your day and please try not to beat up anyone." Ebonee advised him before she shook his hand and walked back to her office. As much as she would have loved to have stood there and gotten lost in his eyes, she knew that if she stayed there much longer that he would have probably questioned the bead of moisture streaming from her under her skirt. She might've been okay if she was still wearing some panties to catch the flow.

Zaddy Issues

Chapter 5

Game Time

The day of the game Trevor arrived on time as planned. Ebonee had already alerted Candace of her date and that she would be dining in as a customer and not her boss. She made sure that Candace was the only one to serve them. When Trevor walked in, Ebonee was already sitting at a table waiting for him. Ebonee showed Candace a picture of Trevor so that she could recognize him when he came inside. As soon Trevor walked in Candace was Johnny on the spot to greet him. She walked him to the table where Ebonee sat. "Hey you!" Ebonee said to Trevor as he was walking up. "Well, look at you. You look even more beautiful in person" he told her as he stretched his arms out for a hug. The two embraced for a moment then took a seat. "Would you two like to order something to drink while you look over the food menu?" Candace asked the two. "I will have a Whiskey Sour" Ebonee requested. "And I'll take an Old Fashion please" Trevor ordered. "I can't tell you how many times I've driven past here and said to myself 'one day I'm going there.' But I have to admit, I didn't imagine that I would be wearing a pair of True Religion Jeans, a Panthers jersey and

Zaddy Issues

sneakers" Trevor confessed as he surveillance the room in admiration. "Oh yeah? What did you imagine yourself wearing then?" she questioned. He looked around at some of the customers and slightly leaned his head in the direction of a couple sitting a couple of tables over from them and said "it definitely wouldn't be a polo shirt and some khakis like that guy. I probably would have at least thrown on a pair of slacks and sports jacket with a nice button down with no tie of course. And I damn sure wouldn't be wearing a pair of shit kickers like the ones he's wearing. I'm sure I would have on my favorite pair of loafers. I feel so underdressed right now" he answered with a chuckle at the end. Ebonee smiled and said, "you look fine and when I say 'fine', it's really an understatement." Trevor blushed and said "Thank you. You look great also."

Candace returned with their drinks to find the two of them gazing into each other's eyes. "Here we go one Whiskey Sour and one Old Fashion. Are you ready to order your food now or will you need to look at the menu a little longer?" Candace asked. "I'll have the Venison and vegetable medley" Ebonee ordered. "That sounds delicious. How's the Grilled Salmon dish here?" Trevor asked as he quickly studied the menu. "It's one of my favorites. But don't take my word for it. Ask boss lady" Candace responded then quickly realized that she'd made the mistake of letting the cat out of the bag. She was so embarrassed that she nervously said "I...I'm so sorry. It slipped." Ebonee was stuck with a blank stare on her face. "It's okay. I Googled the restaurant last night. I know she's the owner" Trevor confessed with a smile. A look of relief fell across Candace's face with Trevor's confession. Candace's expression quickly went from relief to uncertainty when she noticed that Ebonee's blank stare was even more present than before. "Ok...so I'll get these menus out of your way and get your orders into the kitchen where I'll be spending the rest of my shift reliving the moment my career went down the drain" Candace announced and scurried away shaking her head at her own blunder. "Sorry about that. I just.... you...you know I...I just..." Ebonee stuttered as she tried to find the right words to explain what just transpired. Before she could get her words together Trevor reached across the table and placed his hand on Ebonee's then said in a comforting voice, "It's fine. I get it. I too am a little cautious about letting some people know specifics about my line of work and especially my clientele. People automatically start to think that either I have money or can get some tickets for them. Which both are kind of true. I usually can get tickets to almost any sporting event. I'm not rich but not struggling for money either. I have made some pretty lucrative investments outside of my training business that are thriving. I do pretty well for myself financially. So, you don't have to put a clutch your purse on my account. Trust me, I make great money. But...like I said...I get it. And I'm glad it's finally out in the open" Ebonee was sort of ashamed of her behavior but relieved as well.

After eating they had some time to spare before the game started. They ordered another round of drinks to pass the time. The conversation and vibe was everything that Ebonee was accustomed to but even better in person. It was something about being able to look at Trevor's alluring smile that was captivating. He had his locks pulled to the back and tied with another lock. It was hard to tell which sparkled more, his teeth or his hazel-colored eyes when he smiled. She was so lost in his appeal that she found herself not even paying attention to what he was saying. All she could think about was how soft his lips looked and how they would feel against both sets of her lips. Trevor was oblivious to the thigh clinching that was going on across from him. She had Facetimed with him numerous times but having him within reach added a different element of seduction to the conversation. If only he knew just how badly she wanted him, he might would be willing to skip the game. While

Zaddy Issues

sipping on her drink Ebonee got a little choked up when she recognized a familiar face walk through the door. It was Malcolm and he was looking even more dashing than before. This time he wasn't alone. He was accompanied by a beautiful and much younger woman. "What do you say we head out of here after we finish these" Ebonee suggested. Trevor was completely unaware of Ebonee's attempt to avoid having to watch the man that she once lusted over having dinner with another woman. Not only was he with another woman but she looked to b even younger than Ebonee. She also knew that as long as they stayed that she would eventually get caught gazing in Malcolm's direction. "Yeah, we probably should be heading out anyway. The crowd outside is starting to get thick" Trevor agreed looking out of the window to the street. The sidewalks and streets were beginning to fill up with fans of the game. They finished off their drinks and headed for the door. Their clearest path led straight past the table Malcolm and his guest were sitting at. Ebonee had no desire to feel obligated to stop and speak. If they continued there was no way that she could not stop and acknowledge his presence after the way, he stood up for her. But now just wasn't the time. Ebonee stopped walking several feet before reaching Malcolm's table. She turned to Trevor and said "Hey I need to speak with Candace before I leave. Do you mind waiting for me up front?" Trevor nodded and headed to the front. Ebonee made a b-line towards the kitchen. Her retreat was swift, but it didn't go unnoticed. Malcolm spotted her midway to the kitchen. Ebonee made it to the kitchen unaware that Malcolm saw her. She found Candace helping prep food for the cooks. Ebonee walked up to Candace and said, "Hey do you remember the older guy that was in here the other day ready to whoop up on that racist bastard?" Candace grinned and said "Who the zaddy with the beard? Girl hell yeah! We ALL remember him. Shiiiiiit I was thinking about him just yesterday. Why?" Ebonee rolled her eyes and responded, "Do you need a glass of water Ms. Thirsty?" Candace leaned back and said "Ugh…excuuuuse me. I'm just saying. He can get it. You knooow? Of course, you do. I saw how you were all smiles when ya'll were talking. But why do you ask?" Ebonee blushed and said "Whatever! He's in the dining area with another woman. So put your panties back on and make sure that whatever they order is on the house." Ebonee exited the kitchen on the opposite side of the restaurant to avoid having to face Malcolm and his guest.

The rest of the evening was picture perfect. After the game they stopped at a bar and had a couple of drinks more. Neither wanted the night to end but they both had to work

Zaddy Issues

the next morning. They agreed that their next date on that upcoming Saturday would have to be longer. Although they had plans to see each other again in a few days Ebonee was a little surprised that Trevor didn't try to shoot his shot at going back to his place or hers. However, she was kind of happy that he didn't because she probably would have agreed. It had been a long time since she had actually been with a man and the alcohol that had started kicking in wasn't helping any. As much as she really wanted Trevor to take her somewhere and bend her over, she also didn't want to appear to be easy. So, she rushed home to her stash of faithful toys in her nightstand drawer. She texted Trevor once she got home instead of calling. She knew that a phone call would prolong her agenda. She was way too hot and bothered to spend time on what could potentially be an hour or more long conversation. She had business to handle. After a quick shower she jumped in the bed and reached for one of her favorites. She was so horny that as soon as the head of the dildo touched her, she immediately gasped. The massively thick rubber was full of lifelike veins that were raised from the surface. She could feel every one of them as she eased it inside of her. Slowly she penetrated her lubricating walls with half of the ten-inch pleaser. Her nipples were tingling and in desperate need of some attention

Zaddy Issues

as well. She used her free hand to slightly twist and squeeze on her right one while she used her left hand to continue guiding her bulky fake dick in and out. She would have given anything for that to had been Trevor inside of her. She rolled her hips around in the bed with visions of Trevor lying on top of her. She imagined that he was looking into her eyes as she pushed more of the solid black toy deeper. Her walls were squeezing so hard that she could feel the head pressing inside of herself. It felt so good that she couldn't resist biting and licking her nipple for even more pleasure. The feeling of her tongue made her wetter than her shower. The pressure to cum was building but she was going to have to change positions in order to get the feeling that she was looking for. Ebonee got on her knees in the bed and bent over with her hands between her thighs to get the best penetration from the floppy hunk of rubber dick. As it was entering her throbbing walls, a vision of none other than Malcolm invaded her mind. She imagined his hands holding her by the waist filling her with all of the dick that she needed. "Why can't I stop thinking about him" she thought to herself. She had just had a wonderful evening with Trevor. But somehow this man twice her age keeps finding his way into her head. She tried focusing on Trevor but that only made things worse. Now she was thinking about fucking them both at the same time. It was a fantasy that could never come to be. But in her head at that moment, Malcolm was behind her digging deep inside of her while she had a mouth full of Trevor. That was even sluttier behavior than any of her past college experiences. This was going to require breaking out the big guns. She was way too horny for her regular ritual. She reached into her drawer and pulled out her faithful vibrating rose. It was a silicone rose with multiple vibrating modes and a hole in the top for a little suction action that guaranteed a good squirt. Those roses had been trending on the internet for its ability to take women to a climax like none other. She got one to see what the hype was all about, and it never let her down. She arched her back and reached as far between her legs as she needed to reach her throbbing clit with her rose. She didn't want to cum too fast, so she started out on what was considered to be the "low" setting. But in actuality it's so powerful that Ebonee was too afraid to try anything past "medium" speed. That was even more than she would need most times. Slowly she lowered her hips until her arm was securely snug between her body and the bed to keep her hand in place. "Ooh shit!" she moaned as the rose began to work its magic. It didn't take long for her to start rocking back and forth on her toy with the image of Malcolm behind her. She could almost imagine his huge hands gripping her cheeks while he penetrated her. She also imagined how it would feel to have Trevor inside of her mouth at the same time. She wanted so badly to have them both take her body for their own pleasures. The more she imagined the wetter she became. The constant vibration from the rose was making her body heat up into a sizzling ball of lust. She hit the button on the rose to increase the mode to medium where she liked it. "Mmmm..." she moaned even louder than before. The suction from the rose was stimulating her clit while the vibrations were sending shockwaves down her spine. The sensation was so strong that she began to clinch her cheeks uncontrollably. In her mind she had officially slutted completely out. It was so mind blowing that she exploded and came all over the rose. "Aaaaaugh!" she screamed out as cum continuously squirted onto her hand splashing all over the bed until her body collapsed.

Chapter 6

The Definition of A Zaddy

Saturday morning Ebonee and the girls had a day of getting their nails done and shopping. When they were finished, they ventured back to Uptown Cuisine for lunch before Ebonee needed to begin preparing to meet Trevor. As they were finishing their meal Candace walked up to their table. "Hey boss lady. Hey ladies" Candace said to everyone. "Hey girl. Those are some cute earrings you're rocking" Gina pointed out to Candace. "Thank you. That means a lot coming from you. I know you know what you are talking about. I was just telling my homegirl…" Candace continued with a big smile before she was interrupted by Ebonee. "Ummm…did you need something?" Ebonee asked Candace. "Oh yeah…yeah…yeah!" she answered as she quickly turned her attention back to Ebonee. "I meant to tell you but remember the other night when Zaddy Malcolm was here? He left his business card here for you to give him a call" Candace continued with her hand extended with the card. "And you are just now giving it to me? I swear just as soon as I can find a good replacement…" Ebonee joked as she took the card. Candace leaned over and gave Ebonee a

Zaddy Issues

big hug and said "Now you know you ain't gonna find anyone better than me. Stop it! Besides you weren't here most of the day. By the time you came in I was on my way out." Nicole cleared her throat to get attention and said "Um excuse me. I don't mean to break up yawl's little boss slash mentor thing ya'll have going on right now. But ummm...who in the hell is Zaddy Malcolm?" Gina balled up her face and said, "More importantly, what in the hell is a zaddy?" they all looked at Gina in disbelief in her lack of knowledge in current urban lingo. "You're so green!" Nicole pointed out rolling her eyes at Gina. "A 'Zaddy' is what old folks back in the day used to call a 'silver fox'. But now they're called zaddies" Nicole advised. Gina was still looking confused, so Candace added, "a 'Zaddy' is the equivalent to an older man being a 'cougar' like older women are. You know kind of like Ms. Nicole." The look of shock on the three ladies was simultaneous. Nicole threw her head back and said "I know damn well this little heifer didn't just call me a cougar. I know good and damn well she didn't do that." Candace looked puzzled and said "My bad! I thought that was a compliment. I mean ya'll look good for ya'll age though." Nicole rolled her eyes and said "Look a here you little witch. I'm only about ten years older than

Zaddy Issues

you!" Candace looked surprised and said "Dang is that all? I meant…you know…I'm sorry!"

Gina broke the awkwardness by asking "So tell us more about this Zaddy. Hell, I'd like to see him the way you two were grinning. Candace smiled and said "Well wish no more because all you have to do is look over there at the bar. He's been sitting over there waiting to talk to boss lady." They all turned towards the bar at the same time. "Why are you just now telling me" Ebonee questioned. "Well Ms. Gina started complimenting me on my earrings and stuff. Then we all started talking. You know?" Candace exclaimed. Ebonee shook her head and said, "Go let him know that I'll be over there in a moment." "Yes ma'am!" Candace responded. She turned to walk away but was stopped by Nicole. "Oh no the hell not. You go tell him that she is over here, and he can bring his fine ass over here. I need to get a close up" Nicole strongly suggested. "See…that's a cougar move right there. I'm just playing…I'm juuust playing" Candace joked as she scooted away laughing. "Uma hurt that little girl if she keeps playing with me" Nicole jokingly threatened. "So, we still don't know who this Zaddy man is. Are you sleeping with some old man?" Gina questioned. "Ok I know Officer Kareem has probably been teaching you some of his interrogation skills, but I don't know anything about the man

Zaddy Issues

officer" Ebonee sarcastically responded. "First of all, it's Detective Nelson. You need to put some RESPECK on his name. Okaaay?" Gina said in her attempt to show some lost hood side. "And you still didn't say whether or not if you are sleeping with some Bill Cosby dude or not." Gina continued with sincerity. "Bill Cosby? Really? Did you not see what I saw sitting over there at the bar? THAT'S no damn Bill Cosby. He doesn't need any pills to get some coochie. I promise you that." Nicole argued in Malcolm's defense.

Before Gina could respond Malcolm was just a few feet away and quickly approaching their table. Malcolm walked up to the table and said, "Good afternoon, ladies." He turned to Ebonee and said "Forgive my intrusion but the young lady said that it would benefit me more to come over. I didn't want to be rude of course. But I wasn't aware that you would be enjoying time with your friends when I came obviously. If you'd prefer, I can come back another time that you're not with your friends." The sound of his voice gave her that familiar tingle that she experienced the first time that she heard him speak. "No need to apologize. I saw you in here this past Thursday with your lovely wife. I told Candace to make sure to take good care of you. Was everything satisfactory?" Ebonee asked. Malcolm chuckled and said "My daughter and I found everything more than satisfactory.

Zaddy Issues

Thanks." The look on Ebonee's face was nowhere nearly as cracked as it was when he continued with "my wife passed away many years ago." Nicole tossed her napkin on her plate and looked off in disbelief. Gina's jaw dropped and Ebonee gasped. "I'm SO sorry! I forgot that you told me that when we first met. Please forgive me" Ebonee pleaded. He just smiled and said "It's quite alright. We get that sometimes until people take a good look at us and can see the resemblance. But I came back to speak to you about catering her wedding and some other possible business arrangements." Ebonee cleared her throat to gather her words and said "Sure...sure! We can definitely schedule a time to talk. I'm available pretty much all-day next Monday. I'd have to go check with my assistant Candace to see what time would best work for you. If you could just follow me to find her..." Malcolm held his hand out to stop Ebonee from getting out of her seat and suggested "No I can find her and set a time with her. You stay here with your friends and let me take care of it. That's if you don't mind." Nicole sat up in her seat to cross her legs and mumbled "Lord Jesus" under her breath before taking down the rest of her mimosa. Gina on the other hand was still stuck with her mouth open until Nicole motioned for her to close it. Ebonee was nearly in a daze. "Yes Zad...I mean sure. That's fine!" Ebonee replied

Zaddy Issues

as she caught herself nearly making the mistake of calling Malcolm, Zaddy. "Very well then. I look forward to seeing you again sometime on Monday. You ladies enjoy the rest of your day." he said before walking away to find Candace. The three of them sat and watched Malcolm walk away as if they were watching a romance movie. "Giiiirl…GIRL! What in the hell kind of old school GQ model just happened? He was Idris Elba, Barack Obama, Denzel Washington and Dwayne "The Rock" Johnson all rolled up in one! And if THAT'S what a Zaddy is then how do I turn Kareem into one?" Gina joked. Ebonee laughed until she noticed Nicole gathering her things. "What you doing?" Ebonee asked Nicole. "Biiiitch! I'm going by Neiman Marcus to get Anthony one of them Zaddy hats then I'm going HOME!" Nicole answered. "Home? Why? You haven't finished your food." Ebonee questioned. "WHY? What you mean WHY? That man got my cootie cat purring so loud right now. Hooon…eeeey, I'm going home to put this thang all over Anthony. Talking about some why." Nicole responded with conviction while still putting her things in her purse. "Yeah, Kareem is off today, and the kids are with his sister. I'm going home and make him arrest me. I'm trying to get handcuffed now. Thanks to your Zaddy." Gina added. "So ya'll are just going to leave me? Just like that huh?" Ebonee

Zaddy Issues

questioned the two. They both looked over at Malcolm talking to Candace then turned to each other then back to Ebonee and at the same time said "Yep!" Ebonee looked over at Malcolm also and waved goodbye to him as he started to walk off from Candace. "Ok fine. I get it. He got me too right now. Just go!" Ebonee confessed. "Yeah well, I was going anyway. Let us know how tonight goes with Trevor." Nicole requested. "Shit! I almost forgot about Trevor. I need to get out of here myself." Ebonee mumbled.

Chapter 7

Date Night

Ebonee was getting dressed for her date with Trevor when her phone rang. "Hey girl" she answered. "Heeeey! Listen, I know you're probably getting all cute and shit for your date so I'm not going to keep you. BUT…I just need to know a couple of things before you leave. What time are you leaving? And where are you going? Because you don't know this man for real for real. And I'm not trying to look up and see you on the news missing. I need some answers before you go." Nicole asked. Ebonee laughed and said "I feel you, but he's been nothing less than a sweetheart so far. I still don't know where we're going yet. He's supposed to hit me soon with the address where he wants to meet. But trust me; I'm going to Google Map search it first before I go. And besides, I'm going to share my location with you and Gina both anyway." Before Nicole could respond, Ebonee's text notification rang out from her phone. "As a matter of fact, this him texting me now. Hold on" Ebonee told her. She opened the text and clicked the link for the address and smiled. "You're not going to believe this. He wants me to meet him at Mahogany Vineyards. I've been wanting to go

Zaddy Issues

ever since you told me about the time you and Anthony went." Ebonee exclaimed. "Oh really? Yes, girl that place is really nice. The vineyard is as big as I don't know what. They have acres and acres of grapes growing out there. It's only been open for going on about five years now. Well reopened that is. It had been closed for years. But I heard an heir to the family estate returned to reopen. And it's the largest vineyard in North Carolina now. Aaaand its black owned. Umm hmm! Can you tell we took the tour?" Nicole offered. "I thought you two went to a rooftop wine tasting?" Ebonee questioned. Nicole laughed and said "We did...that time. But we've been a few times now. That place is amazing. I would call it a mansion but it's more like a big ass CASTLE. And the wine? They have one that cost as much as my car note. I had to stick to what we could afford. We did a tasting of all of what they sold...that we could afford. Because those really expensive ones, once you opened it you bought it. Ain't no sampling their Honey. You have to make a payment to taste one of them bad boys. You hear me? But anyway, he was right when he said wear something comfortable, especially shoes. Because like I said that place is huge and there's no telling just how much walking or standing you might have to do. They have something going on all the time there. Ain't no telling what might be going on tonight but I'm sure it's going to be nice. Look don't let me talk your head off. Go ahead and finish getting ready. But I still need you to share your location with me. Have fun and be safe. Love you girlie!" "Love you too" Ebonee responded then texted Trevor that she would be there in an hour or so.

She arrived just as the sun was setting behind the humongous home that Nicole accurately described as what also resembled a castle to Ebonee as well. She pulled into a long winding driveway with rows and rows of grape vines as far as the eye could see on both sides of the driveway. When she pulled up to the house, she immediately spotted Trevor standing next to his black Cadillac Escalade truck. "Wow! You look amazing. All I can say is WOW!" Trevor announced as Ebonee walked up to his opened arms. She gave him a hug and said, "you don't look bad yourself there mister." Trevor smiled at the compliment then grabbed Ebonee by the hand and asked "ready?" She looked towards the house and answered "That's a good question. And guess it all depends. You never told me why we're here." Trevor smiled even more and said "I know. So how about we head inside and find out." With a soft tug, Trevor pulled Ebonee close to him and said "Trust me. You're going to like it." They were so close face to face that she had to fight back the

Zaddy Issues

urge to slip her tongue between is juicy full lips. At that moment she would have followed him anywhere. He had her in a trance and she had him in one as well. The sound of an oncoming guest pulling into the parking area near them is the only thing that broke their gazing. "Ok...I'm ready" Ebonee said softly. They locked arms at the elbow and headed towards the home. At the top of the stairs leading to the house was a beautiful brown skinned well dressed young lady with an iPad. "Good evening and welcome to Mahogany Vineyard. Are you here for our Wine & Win Night?" the young lady asked. "Yes, we are" Trevor answered with a big smile. "Wine & Win?" Ebonee questioned with a look mixed with surprise, confusion and excitement while looking back and forth at Trevor and the young. "Why yes ma'am. Tonight's game lineup consists of: 'From Vine To Wine', 'Wine-Opoly', wine trivia and then finally we have our wine masters' event" the young lady happily answered. "Ok then. This does sound fun" Ebonee expressed.

Trevor reached inside of his blazers inside pocket and pulled out his phone and showed it to the young lady for her to scan his electronic tickets. "See, I told you" Trevor boldly boasted with his chest out with a big smile plastered across his face. "This is our fifth annual year doing this. We've had nothing but success with them so much so that people ask all of the time for us to do them more often. If you love wine and this is your first time coming to one, then you're in for a big treat. This is one of the few opportunities to earn a chance to get huge savings on top shelf wine from here. You can earn what we call 'Wine Bucks'. Wine Bucks are like cash here in our store only. You have a full year to redeem them at anytime. You can buy them in the store and give them as gifts but tonight you can win them by playing games. 'From Vine To Wine' which is a board game that you roll the die, move your cork from vineyard, harvest, crushing, clarification, bottling, and tasting. Along the way, answer trivia questions and taste test with each move. Also, we have 'Wine-Opoly', which is obviously a spin on the game of Monopoly. In Wine-Opoly you can win both Wine Bucks and free glasses of wine while you play. There will also be wine trivia where you can earn Wine Bucks' In the wine masters' event participants are presented with five different wines. They will have to taste, smell and look at the wines to determine the type of wine it is. Food will be provided as well with a wide selection of some of our house specials" the young lady suggested. "I can't wait to get started" Ebonee screeched. "Great. All I need is a photo ID and your signatures on our waivers. It just says that once you enter that should you decide to leave that

Zaddy Issues

you agree to leave your vehicle here until the next morning. An Uber ride will be provided to anywhere within 100 miles from here as well as a return ride back to retrieve your vehicle. Should you decide to refuse the Uber ride, you will have to sign another waiver saying that Mahogany Estates nor any of its affiliated companies are responsible for anything that happens to you nor your vehicle once you leave the grounds" she explained. "Oh wow. You guys are pretty serious huh?" Ebonee questioned while handing over her ID and signing the iPad. "Yeah, the owner is big on not drinking and driving. But you're not going to find a better way in town to spend two hundred dollars per person for this type of experience" she happily recommended before stepping aside to let the couple pass.

Chapter 8

The After Party

The evening was a big hit. Ebonee was surprised to see just how knowledgeable Trevor was about wine. He was one of the top winners in every game. He even took first place in the Wine Masters' Event. She was pleased that he gave her all of his Wine Bucks so that she could combine with hers to buy a rather expensive bottle that she normally wouldn't have purchased with her own money. She was also shocked to see that Trevor had plenty of dance moves to show off when the dance floor opened up after the games. She was glad to see that all of his muscles hadn't made him too stiff to move. By the end of the night, they were glad to have the option of having an Uber to drive them. They were both super tired and feeling rather tipsy. Trevor suggested that they share an Uber ride rather than taking two separate rides. He felt that she shouldn't be riding home alone that late with a stranger. They both agreed that it was not only a good idea but also a chance to talk a little more on the ride. During the ride they sat in the backseat holding hands while they laughed and talked about how much fun they had. When they pulled into Ebonee's condominium parking lot they both

Zaddy Issues

opened their doors. "Give me one second my man. I'm going to walk her to her door, and I'll be right back. I just need a moment" Trevor requested of the driver. The driver looked out of the window at Ebonee then turned back to Trevor and grinned. "I'm not mad at you player! Take your time. I'll be right here" the driver said. Trevor patted him on the shoulder and said "My man. Thanks." Trevor hopped out of the car then headed to Ebonee. Together they walked hand in hand up to her front door. "You know, I thought that I knew just about everywhere there was to live in Charlotte. But I have to admit, I never knew these condos existed out here" Trevor confessed looking around grounds. "Yeah, it's fairly new and not a lot of people come out here. I don't even have any neighbors. But it's really temporary until I find the right place to build a house in the next year or so. I'd like to have something bigger with an upstairs and downstairs. But it'll do for now" Ebonee replied. Trevor smiled and handed Ebonee her bag with her bottle of wine. "I had a great time tonight. I hate that tonight has to end. I can't wait to see you again" he said with a sexy grin. "I really enjoyed myself too. But who says it has to end? It's still early and this bottle isn't going to drink itself." Ebonee responded biting on her bottom lip. "Are you sure?" Trevor asked with one eyebrow raised. "Ebonee nodded her head yes then said, "Unless you have something better to do." Trevor giggled and said "Well I was planning on going home to probably call my date from tonight and talk on the phone about all of the fun we had. Maybe try to plan another one with her. But if you're offering wine then I guess I could hang out here and tell you about how wonderful that I think she is." The sound of his voice resonated throughout her body. It could have been the effects of the wine taking over but she was beginning to feel the moisture building between her legs. "Oh, really now? Well in that case I'd love to hear all about this woman" Ebonee said playing along. "Cool then. Give me one second to let the driver know that he can go, and I'll grab my bottle of wine also" Trevor advised before jogging back to the car.

When Trevor returned Ebonee had already gone inside and left the door open for Trevor to enter. He closed the door behind himself and heard Ebonee in the bedroom saying to him "make yourself at home. The TV remote is on the coffee table. Help yourself. I just need to slip into my wine drinking clothes and I'll be right out." Trevor took his blazer off and laid it across her recliner. He looked around her place and asked "where do you keep your wine glasses and bottle opener? I'll go ahead and pour us a drink." Ebonee stepped out from her bedroom wearing a pair of light blue high cut lounge shorts trimmed in pink and a matching spaghetti string tank top. The tank top had a big picture of a wine glass of the front. On the glass it had "I Love to Wrap Both My Hands Around It and Swallow" printed in bold letters. Ebonee stood in the entranceway of the kitchen and said, "The wine glasses are in the cabinet to the left of the refrigerator and the bottle opener is in the drawer next to the stove." Her large perky nipples poking through the tank top were hypnotizing Trevor. Her golden thick thighs pouring out of her short shorts were just as alluring to him. "So that's your wine drinking outfit?" Trevor pleasingly asked. "Absolutely. It helps everything go down smoothly" she answered in a seductive tone. "Everything huh? Is that right" he devilishly responded. Ebonee turned to walk off then stopped to look back over her shoulder and said "EVERYTHING" equally as devilish. She turned and walked off leaving Trevor fixated on the shimmering satin from the jiggle of her cheeks in her shorts. His mind raced with visions of how he was imaging seeing her without the shorts and tank top. His imagination took him from being excited to being all out hungry for her.

Trevor took the glasses and bottle into the living room with him to join Ebonee on the couch. They talked and drank until they were down to the last two glasses from both bottles. By then the effects of the wine was beginning to kick in. Sitting on the couch with Ebonee's feet in Trevor's lap for him to massage, Trevor was fixated on Ebonee's protruding nipples. "See something you like" she asked. Slightly embarrassed Trevor grinned and said "maybe." With the tip of her index finger Ebonee slowly raised the bottom of her top exposing the buttery smooth skin of her belly. "What about now?" she questioned. He licked his lips and smiled but never said a word. Higher she raised the top flashing the base of her breasts. She paused for a moment then closed her eyes and held her head back. The temptation was overwhelming. Without thinking he eased his hand across the waistband of her shorts on up to naval. Her skin felt like heaven to his fingers. She gasped at the touch of his large hand moving across her body. He made his way up her cleavage and to her rock-hard nipple. "Mmmmm" she moaned. Again, she gasped when Trevor leaned over to gently kiss her on the waist. His free hand caressed the inside of her thigh while his right hand gave her nipple a two-finger massage. Ebonee could hardly keep her body still. Ebonee's grinding led Trevor's hand to her pulsating inner thigh. He rubbed his hand across fluffy pussy lips and could feel the moisture building up. Ebonee's moans grew stronger from his finger stroking her sensitive clit. Trevor moved in closer to position himself between Ebonee's legs. He slid her shorts to the side

Zaddy Issues

and helped himself to her wetness. Ebonee reached out and grabbed the back of Trevor's head and slowly pulled him in for a kiss. His full dark lips pressed up against hers as Trevor's long middle finger entered her. Her walls seemed to melt in his hand by the way she was creaming for him. "Ooooh" she groaned when he curled the tip of his finger upward and pressed against her G-Spot. Ebonee's womanly nectar smothered what started as one finger but quickly increased to two fingers inside of her. His thumb stroked the tip of her clit in a circular motion. The more he stroked the more passionately they kissed. Their tongues clashed against one another with the taste of good wine and desire.

Ebonee reached up and began to unbutton Trevor's shirt for him. She only got two of the buttons undone before he sat up and ripped the shirt completely open for her. Buttons flew everywhere and displayed the most well-defined torso that she had ever seen in person let alone hovering over her. His pecs were the size of two salad plates. His stomach looked like building blocks perfectly stacked on top of one another. His shoulders muscles were like two big balls of chocolate with big chocolate arms attached. He threw the remains of his shirt onto the floor then reached down to help Ebonee out of hers. She willingly leaned forward to allow him to pull it over her head. While sitting up closer to him she took advantage of the opportunity to plant a kiss onto his large chest. Gently she moved across his body kissing and licking him. Trevor placed his hands on her shoulders then laid her back. He pulled her shorts down and off then slung them across the room. He slid onto the floor on his knees then reached his arm behind Ebonee and pulled her around until she was sitting in front of him. He raised her legs up high then draped them across his shoulders. He grabbed her by the hips and pulled her closer to him until her cheeks were at the edge of the couch. He leaned in and scent of her love was even more intoxicating to him than the wine. He opened his mouth and placed her clit underneath his top lip then placed his bottom lip at the bottom of her hole with his tongue slowly licking inside of her. Ebonee grabbed a handful of his locks and took a deep breath with her other hand over her mouth when his tongue met her clit for the first time. Shockwaves shot up her spine from the way his tongue and lips were slurping on her. Over and over, he licked and sucked on her fat clit with his bottom lip brushing against her sopping wet lips. Suddenly he snatched Ebonee even closer until her hips were slightly raised enough for Trevor thrust his tongue deep inside of her. His lips surrounded her juicy little hole as he gave her a tongue fucking like she had never experienced. His dreadlocks bounced around across her stomach and waist as he moved his head all over the place. He was driving Ebonee crazy with his wickedly good tongue work. She couldn't imagine it getting any better until he scooped her short thick body up in his arms then stood up with her. Her legs were still draped across his shoulders with his big hands placed firmly under her fluffy cheeks. He raised her up high enough to continue eating from her as if he was on an island simply drinking from half of a coconut shell on the beach. She went from holding him by his hair to slamming her hands on the ceiling when she felt the uncontrollable urge to explode all over his face. He welcomed every slippery drop from his lips to on down across his robust beard.

He sat Ebonee back onto the couch once she was done thrusting and shaking against his face. "Woooow…that was amazing. I've never had it like that before. I knew you were strong and all but DAMN! That really was AMAZING!" she blissfully confessed. "I'm glad you liked it. I enjoyed it too. And what's amazing is the way you taste. I really didn't want to stop but the way you were squeezing my neck with your thighs I didn't know if I could handle a second round without dropping you" Trevor confessed as well. Ebonee giggled and said "Well you wouldn't have had to worry about dropping me. Because I probably would have had to hop down if you had kept going." Trevor laughed as he used his torn off shirt to wipe off his face and beard. With his face partial covered by the shirt he was unaware that she was reaching for his belt buckle. Slowly he lowered the shirt from his face and looked down to find Ebonee undoing his pants. He dropped the shirt to his side when she reached into his pants and pulled out the biggest surprise of her life. She was expecting much more than what he had to offer. Although she had seen much smaller dicks than his she couldn't help for feeling slightly disappointed. She was a bit let down, but it wasn't enough to stop her at that point. It had been so long since she had actually been with a real man that she was not about to abandon her mission. Besides, with the tongue game he possessed she was still feeling the effects and willing to compromise. Once she got a good grip around him, she placed the head inside of her mouth. It was then that she realized that he may not have had the longest dick she'd ever had but it was definitely one of the thickest. And that was workable for her. She ran her tongue across the tip of his wide mushroom shaped head then sucked him into her mouth like a vacuum. Her lips massaged his shaft while her head bobbed back and forth for his pleasure. Her warm tongue caressed every inch of him. She brought him to his tip toes when she reached between his legs with her right hand then grabbed him by the ass cheek and started forcing him all the way into her mouth. Trevor threw his head back and grabbed Ebonee by the back of her head with both hands when he felt her tongue licking his balls at the same time his dick was in her mouth. He could feel her nose pressed against his stomach. Ebonee moaned in pleasure at the taste of his sweet precum leaking into her mouth. She suddenly found herself extremely aroused again at the way he was responding to the way she was consuming him. "Yes baby! Don't stop!" he begged repeatedly as her head went back and forth with him sliding in and out of her slippery mouth. Gradually she increased the speed until she was gripping his cheeks with all she had and using him to fuck her own face. He tensed up then let out a roar and a load of cum down her throat at the same time. Then he pulled out and shot the rest between her breasts.

"Turn around and bend over" Trevor requested. Ebonee did as told and put her knees in the couch and grabbed onto the back while Trevor finished removing his shoes and pants. He put a condom on then got down behind her with his knees between hers. Gently he eased the wide head of his dick between her perfectly round cheeks until he was able to rub it against her clit. The thickness of his shaft was a feeling that Ebonee was longing. Her walls welcomed him with a

Zaddy Issues

shower of wetness. She could feel him spreading her and stretching her walls open with every gentle plunge. The feeling was good, but she was beginning to want more. She looked back at Trevor and said, "Give it to me!" Faster and harder he pumped until his locks were bouncing all over his head. "YES! THAT'S IT!" she screamed out. "Ooooh SHIT! YES, BABY YES!" she continued. He placed his hands on both of her shoulders fucked her as hard as he could. Ebonee leaned over with her breasts bouncing around over the back of the couch from Trevor constant pounding. He may not have been getting the deepest, but he was definitely hitting all walls and that was feeling good to Ebonee, especially since she hadn't had a man inside of her in months. Her walls were throbbing, and she could feel the cum starting to build. But she wasn't the only one feeling it. Trevor was also getting the overwhelming urge to come again. Ebonee began to bounce her cheeks off of him with extreme force and Trevor was giving as good as he was receiving until they both erupted like volcanoes at the same time. Ebonee came so hard that it poured out of her and onto the couch. Trevor in return filled his condom with a load that surrounded him from the tip to the base of his dick. Exhausted and worn out they stretched out on the couch and passed out in each other's arms.

Zaddy Issues

Chapter 9

Back To Business

After picking up their rides the next day they spent hours on the phone together reliving the night before among other topics. The time Ebonee didn't spend talking to Trevor, she spent it talking with about her date with Trevor. She got a good night's sleep and woke up with some extra pep in her step and decided to head to the restaurant considerably earlier than normal. When she arrived, she was surprised to find a white BMW i7 with tinted windows parked next to her parking space. If there was one thing her father passed down to Ebonee it was his love for luxury cars. And this was no ordinary big body sedan. This was a quarter of a million-dollar vehicle. She pulled into her park and got out of her car. The back passenger window on the driver's side rolled down as she was heading towards the back entrance of the restaurant. "I hope you don't mind me being early" a voice from the car said. She nervously turned to see who was in the car and saw Malcolm sitting inside. "I didn't mean to startle you. I just wanted to catch you before you got inside" he explained. "Startled? Try scared to death. I wasn't expecting to meet with you until sometime after lunch" she affirmed. "This is true. However, I had some other business to come up that I'm unable to reschedule. So, I was hoping that we could meet a little sooner. Like now." Malcolm informed her. "Well, it just so happens I'm here a little early with nothing major to do. I guess I can fit you in for an early meeting. Follow me inside" Ebonee suggested. She motioned for Malcolm to get out then turned back to head towards the backdoor again. "I was actually hoping that you would be willing to take a ride with me while we talked business" Malcolm requested. Ebonee turned back around with a look of shock. "Excuse me?" she questioned. "It's just something about the sound of the city awakening in the morning that I just love. I do some of my best work in here. I promise we won't stay gone long" Malcolm declared. She was a little hesitant at first but then figured she'd never heard of anyone one being abducted in a car worth six figures.

She got in the back next to Malcolm and was immediately greeted with the scent of his expensive cologne. She was instantly mesmerized from not only how he smelled but at how bossy he looked sitting next to her with his legs crossed and hand propped up on his knee displaying a diamond pinky ring. "Thank you for joining me" Malcolm said as Ebonee slid into her seat and closed the door. "This is a really nice car" she said looking around the inside like a child in a toy

Zaddy Issues

store. They pulled off and hit the street. "So, tell me, do you have an idea of a particular type of menu plan you'd like to have for your wedding? And about how many guests are you expecting?" Ebonee politely asked. "Well to be honest, no I don't. I don't have the slightest idea about anything for the menu. But I do know that there will be at least two hundred people attending" Malcolm truthfully responded with a chuckle. "Honestly, I was hoping that you could provide some recommendations. As a matter of fact, I would much rather allow you to create the menu and just let me know how much I will have to pay. And money is no object" Malcolm confessed. "Are you sure? What about food allergies? With two hundred guests you're bound to have someone that is allergic to seafood and some that may not eat pork. We have to consider those people as well" Ebonee suggested. Malcolm thought for a moment then said "I guess you're right. I didn't think about that. The last thing we want is to have someone kill over behind a plate of food. See…that's why I'm leaving it up to you. But as far as the pork, I've never heard of anyone having an allergic reaction to pork like seafood. If you choose a pork dish, then we can also include some kind of poultry dish for those that don't eat pork. But we're not going to just "X" it out unless you choose not to do it. Personally, I love pork. Especially smothered pork chops in gravy. But then again, I am a good ole country boy." Malcolm stated. "Is that so? From your accent I would have taken you for a northerner. But since you said something, I guess I can hear a hint of a twang in there" Ebonee replied. Malcolm smiled and explained, "Ooooh nooo! I'm from right outside of Charlotte. I grew up in Concord as a matter of fact. However, I did spend over thirty years living upstate in New Rochelle, NY. But I've been back and forth to the Queen City now for going on about four or five years now. My father, may he rest in peace started getting ill from prostate cancer a few years back and was having difficulties maintaining the family business. Things got so far out of control that he came close to losing everything that he had worked so hard for many years. My younger brother was helping him rebuild while I was in New York but then he got sick with COVID-19 and passed away. We all took it pretty hard but none like my father. I guess it was a good thing that my mother had passed back when we were teenagers. She would have been worse than my father. Two months later my wife passed away from COVID as well. It was six months to the date after losing my wife that my father's doctor told him he had maybe six months to live. The cancer had spread and pretty much consumed my father's entire body. Six months turned out to be two weeks and he was gone. Just like that. So, after I buried my father, I realized that I didn't want to stay in a house that held so many heartbreaking memories that I decided to make a new start in an old familiar place. My kids were all grown up and moved out of the house. I really didn't have anything keeping me there. I owned my own real estate company with offices in New York, New Jersey, Delaware and Connecticut that are all pretty self-operated. So, I figured I'd move back down south to expand as well as pick up where my father left off."

When he was done talking, Ebonee was left with her jaw dropped. She clung to his every word as if she was watching it all play out in front of her. "Wooow! What an amazing story. I'm heartbroken for all of your losses but I'm also happy for you about your new start. I don't even know what to say at this point" Ebonee said sitting back in her seat astonished at his life. She was so caught up that she hadn't even noticed that they had gotten off of the highway and headed towards Lake Norman. They eventually pulled into a neighborhood that was still under development. Most of the homes were still under construction but several were either finished or just a few steps away from being finished. Although there was still a lot of work to be done it wasn't hard to tell by the sizes of the yards and homes that it was not for the under privileged. It was expected to spend mid to high six figures for most lakeside homes but every house there was easily worth seven to eight figures. Ebonee speechlessly surveyed the area with her jaw dropped once again until she realized Malcolm was amused at watching her. Ebonee gathered her composure and asked, "Ok so do you mind telling me where we are and why we're here?" Before Malcolm could answer her the car pulled up to a driveway with a large black wrought iron fence that surrounded the large front yard so far that she couldn't even see where it ended. The driver entered a code on the keypad in front a huge gate with fancy golden initials "M" on the left and "C" on the right that led to the biggest home in the neighborhood. "William pull around to the back for me please" Malcolm ordered his driver. The older gentleman behind the wheel never turned around nor uttered a word. He just nodded and did as told. Malcolm turned to Ebonee and asked, "Remember when I asked you for this meeting, I said I may have some other business opportunities?" "Yes. Is this where you're planning to host the wedding or something?" she responded. He smiled and said "Oh no. This entire neighborhood is one of my projects. I bought all of this undeveloped land and created 'Hollie Grove'. As they pulled around to the back of the house Ebonee spotted beautiful

Zaddy Issues

boat at the end of the backyard tied to his personal dock in the lake. "And THIS...this is MY house" he said full of pride. "I will admit, this is nice. I mean reeeal nice. But again, why are we here?" Ebonee asked before she allowed herself to get caught dumbfounded again by everything. Malcolm adjusted himself in his seat so that he could face Ebonee more. He said "This is my dream home. I have others but this is the one that I've dreamt of since I was a child. And my vision for my dream house is to have a restaurant style kitchen in it. I don't need a full-size restaurant kitchen but more of a condensed version of one. And I didn't want to just hire any old architect or designer. I wanted someone with real five-star quality experiences to help me bring my vision to life. I'd like for you to design it as if it was your own and you had unlimited range to do whatever you wanted. I feel like if I had someone that was passionate about their kitchen to help that they would bring an element of that passion and love to the design of my kitchen too. So, if you would do me the honor of providing your personal influence, I think that I could make my dream kitchen a reality. And of course, I will pay you well for your work." Ebonee became a little excited at how intimately he spoke about his vision. He had a way of captivating her when he spoke. She cleared her throat and said, "Well since you put it that way, let's see what it looks like inside now."

They got out of the car and left the driver William in the car alone and went inside. The empty home provided the echoing sounds of their heels walking across the marble floor leading into a huge room in the back of the house. "This will be my office space once I have everything completed. The view of the lake from here is relaxing. I need that sometimes when I'm trying to handle business." Ebonee walked up to the large cathedral style window that led from the floor to the top of the high ceiling. She gazed out at the lake and said "I see what you mean. This is a beautiful view." "Yes…it is a very beautiful view from here" he responded while standing only a couple of feet behind Ebonee. Not sure if he was actually talking about the view of the lake or the view of her from behind, her body spontaneously tensed up. She glanced over her left shoulder to find Malcolm with both of his hands in his pants pockets looking debonair in his suit and no tie. "Are you ready for more? If not, we can stay right here as long as you want. I could stay in it all day." Malcolm suggested. "Excuse me" Ebonee questioned. "This room…this view. I could stay in here all day. But I know you have things to do. Let me show you the rest of the house and then we can come back downstairs to the kitchen area on our

Zaddy Issues

way out" he answered knowing that he was caught slipping. Ebonee gave him the "ummm hmmm" look with a little crooked smile as she walked past him to head out of the room. She knew then that he was definitely referring to her as the view he was enjoying, and it sent a throb to her panties. He took her up the winding staircase to view the theater room, bedrooms, and everywhere else. The whole time Ebonee was imagining Malcolm having his way with her in each room they entered. By the time they made it back down to the kitchen she was so hot and bothered that she had begun to sweat a little. Finally, they entered this large open space that was the unfinished kitchen. There weren't even any cabinets in there yet. "You weren't kidding when you said that you were looking to start from scratch. And even though you're not looking for a restaurant size kitchen, you have more than enough space for one. This is going to be fun." She said with excitement at the amazing opportunity. "So does that mean you'll do it?" Malcolm asked in shock. Ebonee looked around the open space then nodded her head and said "What the hell? Yeah…I'll do it. I'm already seeing lots of potential. Let's do it!" Malcolm's eyes lit up with excitement. "I really appreciate this. You have made my day. But there're just a couple of other things that I'm going to need in order to make this work" he said. "What do you need?" she asked. He clapped his hands together and clinched them tightly then said "I need you to teach me how to cook. I don't want to have this big gourmet style kitchen and my signature dish is fried chicken and canned vegetables. With all that I have going on I don't really have the time to enroll in a class. Plus, it will technically be your kitchen and I'd rather learn from the person that specially designed my kitchen. I know you're a busy woman as well. So, I obviously would pay you twice the cost of whatever the tuition that I would have to pay a school for your…personal lessons." Ebonee blushed knowing that he obviously had a hidden agenda that she was becoming more and more aligned with than he realized. "That might be doable. What do you have in mind in terms of days and hours?" she asked. Malcolm grinned and said "You tell me. I can be available for a couple of hours any weekday after six in the evening." Ebonee grinned back biting her bottom lip and said "I'm thinking maybe every other Tuesday and Thursday should work for me. When do you think you might be able to get started?" Malcolm threw his hands up and asked "What about this week. Tomorrow is Tuesday." Ebonee took a quick spin in a circle looking around with her hands out asking "And how are we supposed to do that? You don't have anything in here." Malcolm laughed and said "Of

Zaddy Issues

course not here. This isn't my only home. Remember?" Ebonee dropped her head laughing and said "I forgot who I was talking to for a second there. But I can't start tomorrow. I have plans. But I can start Thursday. If that's okay with you." They shook hands to seal their agreement then headed back to the car for Malcolm to give Ebonee a ride back to the restaurant for work.

Chapter 10

Girl Talk

All day at work Ebonee couldn't help for thinking about the time she spent with Malcolm that morning. Even after work she couldn't wait to get home to jump on a three-way call with the girls. She was itching to tell someone other than Candace about her morning. When she got home, she went ahead and prepared dinner since she had to wait for Gina and Nicole to get home from work anyway. She didn't want either of them to get distracted or pulled away from their conversation by one of their husbands' or children. She needed their undivided attention for this kind of tea. This was no ordinary mason jar drinking tea. This was that richly sweet southern type of tea that you serve up in your good china and drink with your pinky finger in the air. After eating she found an old episode of "Law & Order" to watch while she waited to make her calls. Not even ten minutes into the show her phone began to ring. It was Trevor. "Well, hello there sir. How are you doing?" she answered. "I can't complain. I had you on my mind and thought I'd give you a call. How was your day?" he responded. He had no idea just how long she'd been waiting and yearning to tell someone all about her day. But there was no way she could disclose everything to Trevor. "It was rather eventful actually" she responded with a giggle. "Oh really? Tell me all about it" Trevor requested with genuine excitement. It took all that she had not to spill everything to him. But she knew that was a conversation for the girls. She really wanted to rush Trevor off of the phone so that she could get to the real call that she'd been waiting all day to make. "Well, I had a really good meeting with a client that wants my restaurant to cater a two hundred guests wedding for his daughter that I feel may open some doors for me in the future. He also hired me to help with designing a restaurant quality kitchen in one of his homes. If all goes well these opportunities could move my house buying up by months. I'm really excited about this" she emphatically expressed. "That sounds amazing. I'm sure you're going to knock it out of the park" Trevor encouraged. Then Ebonee's phone beeped with another call on the other line. "Hey, my girl Gina is beeping in. Can I hit you later? I've been waiting on this call" she asked. "Go ahead and take it. I'm actually going to take it down early tonight. I have an early day tomorrow. Have a good night" he explained.

They said their goodbyes then Ebonee quickly clicked over to catch the call. "GIRL! You're not going to believe the kind of morning that I had TODAY! But first I need to call Nicole and get her on three-way so that…" Ebonee started say. But before she could finish, she was interrupted. "Child I'm already on here" Nicole responded. "Oh good. Do ya'll remember the older guy that came over to our table the other day?" she asked. "Who Zaddy Malcolm? Hell yeah! What's up?" Nicole asked. "Ya'll talking about that old man with the swag?" Gina added. Ebonee popped her lips and said "Yaaaaaas! That's the one. Girl I was supposed to have a lunch meeting with him today. How about this man was in the restaurant's parking lot this morning waiting on me…in a white i7…with a DRIVER? I was like oh my God" Before she could go any further with her story Gina blurted out "Ok you need to calm down. First of all, I don't know what no i7, j7, b7 or any other 7's. Sounds like you're talking about BINGO! But I'm guessing you're talking about some kind of expensive car. But hell, he's probably too old to drive anyway." Nicole took a deep sigh and said "See…that's why we can't take your country ass anywhere. An i7 is BMW car. And if you own one then you can afford a driver." Ebonee quickly jumped back in with "THANK YOU Nicole. Now as I was saying, he came this morning and instead of having our meeting inside of the restaurant he took me to his house." Without missing a beat Gina gasped then asked "Did you

Zaddy Issues

give that old man some pussy? You can mess around and give that old man a heart attack with all that badonka donk you got. And you know they say old men will give you worms you know?" Nicole was getting obviously annoyed with Gina's outbursts. "Will you please be quiet and let the woman speak. Besides, that worm shit is just an old wives' tale probably started by some old bitch that hadn't had any dick in years and had to come up with an excuse. And so, what if she did. He looked like he had some snake to give. Damn some worms. Go on Eb. And Gina hush!" Nicole argued.

After Nicole put Gina's interruptions to an end Ebonee was able to finish telling them about her morning with Malcolm in peace. But as soon as Ebonee finished Gina took the opportunity to jump back in with "Well it sounds like it was a good meeting, but it also sounds like you're gonna end up giving him some anyway. All I'm going to tell you is if it last longer than four hours, do like the warning label says and call a doctor. Because you know he probably keeps a pocket full of Viagra. Don't let him Kevin James you. He mess around and wake up dead. Then what?" Once again Nicole stepped in with "First of all you mean Kevin Samuels. And again, so what if she gives him some. You're so old-fashioned when it comes to men and relationships. I feel sorry for poor Kareem. You probably don't even get on top. I bet you probably even be on ya phone Tik Toking while that man is trying to be intimate. Just no excitement in bed." Gina giggled at Nicole and said, "I'll have you know that my man is very satisfied and doesn't mind if I Tik Tok as long as he gets his." Ebonee and Nicole both burst into laughter at Gina. "Is that what you think?" Nicole questioned. "That's what I know. He ain't gone anywhere and he's NOT going anywhere. Thank you!" Gina snapped. "Oh, calm down girl. We're just messing with you. We know Kareem be handcuffing you and shit" Ebonee said trying to bring a little laughter back into the conversation. "Yeah, we know you're the same uuuusual suspect assuuuuuming the expected position" Nicole sarcastically added with a laugh. The three of them fell out laughing with Gina laughing the hardest. "I can't stand yo ass. That's why Candace called you a cougar. And Ebonee yo ass is gonna end up having to change his diapers. You need to stick with Trevor and leave that old man alone if you know like I know." That's when Ebonee became aggravated. "You act like I'm in a relationship with either of them. And who said that I was going to sleep with Malcolm? And if I do then that's my business. And Trevor is a good guy and all, but I need more" Ebonee exclaimed. Quickly Gina responded with "Trevor is closer to your age. He has a good job. He thinks the world of you and he's fine as HELL. What more could you want?" "DICK BITCH! She needs more dick from him and he ain't got it and CAN'T get it! Do you not remember her telling us last night about how short his dick was? Come on now. The girl wants more dick...the fuck!" Nicole responded for Ebonee. "There's more to a man than dick Nicole" Gina debated. "Yeah, but good dick is also important. And don't get me wrong, it's not that he didn't please me sexually, but I don't know." Ebonee revealed. "I don't see the problem then" Gina doubled down. "DICK...DAMN! I'm getting off the phone and going to get me some cause you crazy. Ya'll have a good night" Nicole said just before hanging up. "Look I know you. And I know that you want a man that is going to be your everything but honey sometimes you have to compromise. Don't let a little dick keep you from being with a man that checks all of the other boxes. And when I say 'little dick' I mean that both literally and figuratively. There's more to a healthy relationship than just 'DICK' as Ms. Dick Thirsty herself Nicole puts on. Trevor is a good catch and should seriously consider that. There's not a lot of Trevors' out there. Just think about it is all I'm saying. But I'm going to get off of here too. Goodnight sweetie." Gina

Zaddy Issues

offered before hanging up also. Ebonee was left feeling like they both had good points and gave her a lot to sleep on.

Chapter 11

Culinary Arts 101

Ebonee and Trevor spoke throughout the week and planned to go out that Saturday. After nearly a week to think about her advice from Gina, she found herself excited about giving Trevor another chance at sparking something more than what he had to offer in bed, but she was also just as excited about her first cooking class with Malcolm. That Thursday afternoon she received a text from Malcolm with the address where to come and for a list of things that he would need. After several texts back and forth with Malcolm confirming that he was properly prepared she was beginning to feel like she may have been reading more into their relationship than it really was. The last thing that she wanted to do was make a fool out of herself and blow an opportunity of a lifetime by being promiscuous. Millions of women across the country would kill for an opportunity like this. She didn't want to ruin it with the assumption that she was hired strictly for a chance to be some old man's fling. Too many women in the "Me Too Movement" had sacrifice far too much to fall victim as well. She was torn between the two possibilities to the point that she was unfocused most of the day at work.

Zaddy Issues

Eventually she ended up leaving earlier than usual. She needed time to get herself mentally prepared as well as finding something to wear. She didn't want to arrive wearing anything too suggestive. But with curves like hers it wasn't going to be an easy task. Once she got home, she was ironically able to find a pair of grey sweatpants that usually in the case of men would be presumably suggestive to say the least. But with an oversized matching sweatshirt she figured there was no way that this could come off as otherwise. It was the least sensual outfit that she owned. She even decided not to wear any makeup to assure not to give off any kind of vibe less than professional.

She pulled up to the address she was given for a house that was every bit as big as the one he was having built. She walked up to the door and rang the doorbell. "Just a second" she heard Malcolm yelling from inside. Malcolm opened the door with a big smile and said "Come on in. I was just in the kitchen laying out everything that you asked for." She felt a lot better when she saw that he too was dressed down and not in one of his expensive suits. Nevertheless, she was just as attracted to him in his jeans and Hugo Boss t-shirt. She also never would have imagined him in a pair of sneakers and a fitted Yankees cap. It was an expensive thuggish look that only he could pull off without appearing to try to look young. "Let me take your jacket" he asked with his hand out. She walked in then took off her jacket and was immediately impressed at how stylish his home was decorated. "That's a really nice baby grand piano. Do you play?" she asked pointing at the piano in a corner. He chuckled and said "Actually it's not a baby grand. It's a Steinway Concert Grand piano that I purchased a few years ago from Carnegie Hall. But like most people, I didn't always know the difference either. And yes, I play a little." Malcolm started walking towards the back of the house and Ebonee followed him passing multiple rooms with closed doors until they reached the kitchen. A large island full of all of the things she needed sat in the middle of the kitchen with two stools on both sides of it. She walked up to the island to inspect everything and smiled. "Looks like you got everything. Good job. Let's get started, shall we?" she advised with her nod of approval. Malcolm snapped his fingers and said "Just one second. I almost forgot. I have something for us. I'll be right back." He dashed off back in the direction of the front door. She could hear him running up the stairs then moments later running back down. He popped back into the kitchen carrying two medium sized gift bags in his hands. He handed one to Ebonee and sat the other one on the island top. "What is this" she asked with a big smile on her face. "Open it and see" Malcolm suggested. She reached inside past the layers of tissue paper and pulled out her gift. It was a black apron that had "Kiss the Cook and Bring Her Wine" printed on the front of it with pictures of a chef's hat, a glass of wine and a lipstick-stained kiss also printed on it. Her smile turned to flew blown laughter. "I love it! Thaaaanks" she shrieked in joy. "I have one for myself as well" Malcolm advised reaching into the other bag. He held his apron up to show Ebonee. The front of his read "That Ain't Burnt, That's Flavor" on the front of it. "Oh my God that is too cute. Put it on and let me help you tie it in the back for you" she gladly offered. He put the top strap around his neck then turned around for her to assist. She took her time tying the strings in the back so that she could admire his backside. "There, now do me" she said then quickly turned around. Realizing how that sounded she quickly turned back around and shamefully said "That didn't come out right." Malcolm laughed and said, "I know what you meant." She smiled and put the top strap around her neck then turned back around for Malcolm to help with her strings. When he finished, he placed his hands on her waist then said "There, you're all set." The feeling of his hands on her body sent a chill down her spine. She was momentarily frozen by his touch. She cleared her throat then took a step forward towards the end

Zaddy Issues

of the island. She turned to Malcolm and said "Ok then. I just need to use the restroom and freshen then we can get started." Malcolm stretched his hand out towards a hallway and said, "It's the second door on the left."

When she returned, she found Malcolm sitting on one of the stools with a bottle of red wine on the island and two wine glasses full of wine waiting on her. "What is this I see Mr. Cox?" Ebonee jokingly asked. Malcolm picked up the glasses and handed one to her when she got within reach. She accepted the glass and Malcolm stood to his feet then held his glass up and said, "Here's to my first day of class and to what I believe is going to be a team for many years to come." They touched glasses then took a sip. "This is delicious" Ebonee expressed. Malcolm smiled and said "The apron said to bring wine to the cook. I'm glad you like it. I have plenty more of where that comes from." Ebonee raised her glass and gave her nod of approval then they took another sip. "All we need now is a little cooking music" Ebonee recommended. "Say less. What type of music would you like to hear?" he asked. "Oh, I don't know. Anything will be fine. Especially if you keep this wine coming" she joked. Malcolm chuckled and advised her "Be careful what you wish for. I'm old school babygirl. I'll have you listening to all kinds of things from the blues to old school eighties or

Zaddy Issues

nineties hip hop. Or I just might hit you with something from Earth Wind and Fire." Ebonee fell out laughing at Malcolm when he started clowning around doing his little two-step while he ran down his list of suggestions. "I don't mind old school, but we don't have to play anything that's going to get you too worked up in here. I don't know CPR" she teased. Malcolm's eyes bucked wide open, and his jaw dropped wide open with a grin. He covered his mouth with his fist and said through his clinched hand "I know you didn't. So, what are you trying to say?" Ebonee held her glass up to her mouth then placed her other hand on her hip and mumbled with a smile "I'm just saying. You know..." Malcolm uncovered his mouth to reach for the hand on her hip. He held her hand up and firmly placed it on his chest and said, "Does it feel like there's a bad heart behind there?" It was then she realized that he was in better shape than she had even previously fantasized. Slowly she slid her hand away taking the time to briefly enjoy the tightness of his muscular frame. It was then too that she noticed just how big and muscular his arms were. It was clear that Malcolm was no ordinary older man. As her father would say "He was cut from a different cloth."

Malcolm pulled his phone out of his pants pocket and said "I have the perfect cooking music. Its old school but the whole

Zaddy Issues

album is a laid-back classic." He clicked a couple of buttons then Frankie Beverly and Maze's song "Southern Girl" started playing through his surround sound system. "Okay. Now I can get with that." Ebonee said bobbing her head and snapping her fingers to the music. She took another sip of her wine then turned her attention to the ingredients on the island. "So, I see you let the duck sit out to dry like I told you. I see you have the oranges. I see the side vegetables. You have all of the spices but where is the honey? We can't make honey glazed duck without some honey. It's practically in the name of the dish" she said as she took inventory. Malcolm held his finger up and said "Aaaah yes. That's the one thing that I didn't have to go out and buy. I guess that's why I forgot to set it out. But I have plenty. I'll get it." He walked over to a huge pantry the size of a small bedroom and opened the door. He stepped inside and came back out with a jar and another bottle of wine then sat them both on the island top. Ebonee grabbed the jar of honey to read the label. "Manuka? What kind of honey is this?" she asked with a confused look on her face. Then a light bulb came on in her head. "Oh wait. I've heard of this kind of honey. This is that freaky honey ain't it?" she asked with her hand covering a big smile. Malcolm was taking a sip of wine and nearly spat it out trying to hold back his laughter. "I

Zaddy Issues

don't know about any freaky honey, but all honey has an aphrodisiac quality. Some are stronger than others. Manuka is considered one that has high qualities but that's not why I have it. I buy it because it tastes better than the local and processed honey. Raw Manuka honey is healthier for you." he explained. Ebonee pressed her lips together and said "Mmmm hmmm. If you say so." Malcolm reached inside of a drawer to the island and pulled out two spoons. He opened the honey and scooped some out with one of the spoons. "Here…taste it. I bet you can tell the difference." He said as he extended the spoon to Ebonee. Jokingly she took the spoon and gave it a little sniff. She placed the spoon in her mouth and instantly started smiling when the richly sweet honey melted on her tongue. "Oh my God. You were right. This is NOT the same as regular honey. I need a little more if you don't mind" she said. Malcolm handed her the jar and said "See…I told you. You can have as much as you like. I have several jars in the pantry. As a matter of fact, I think I'll go get my own jar to eat out of and a jar for cooking." Ebonee laughed then dipped her spoon in the jar and said "That's a good idea because I wasn't planning on sharing. I'm taking this jar with me when I leave. You won't getting it back." Malcolm smiled shaking his head then walked off to the pantry.

Chapter 12

How To Handle Luxury Cars

After eating they sat at the dinner table across from one another for awhile discussing options for the kitchen in the new home. "So, you say you can play that big ole pretty piano in there" Ebonee asked waving her half finished glass of wine in a circular motion. It was clear that the wine was beginning to kick in for both of them. Malcolm sat up in his seat and said, "Do I detect a hint of disbelief?" Ebonee smirked then rolled her eyes and said "I'm just saying...you knooow! Can you play or can you plaaaay plaaaay?" Malcolm took the napkin from his lap then tossed it onto his empty dinner plate and said, "There's only one way to find out right?" He stood up and walked around to Ebonee's side of the table then said, "Follow me!" He held his hand out for her to take it and she did. They walked back into the room with the piano with Ebonee trailing behind him hand in hand. Malcolm took a seat at the piano while Ebonee leaned against it waiting to see what he was going to do. Deep down she never doubted that he could actually play but it wouldn't have surprised her either if he had only said it just to try to impress her. It wouldn't have been the first time that a man lied to her. But Malcolm was far from being like any other man that she had dated in the past. He was mature and sophisticated. Not to mention, he was rich and didn't have a need to lie to get a woman. "So, what would you like to hear?" he asked with a light smile. From the way his eyes were getting low could see that either he was getting himself in concert mode or the wine was kicking in on him too or maybe even both. Regardless to what the cause was he was looking even sexier to Ebonee the way he looked sitting at that piano. "Remember we went through that whole 'what do you want to hear' fiasco earlier in the kitchen? So how about you play whatever is your favorite song to play?" she jokingly suggested. "No problem!" he responded. First came the familiar melodic run of piano notes ringing out through the room. Then Malcolm opened his mouth and sang "I've been so many places in my life and time. I've sung a lot of songs. I've made some bad rhymes…" Not only did he shock her with his piano skills, but she nearly hit the floor when he started to sing also. He was singing Donny Hathaway's classic hit "A Song For You". Unbeknownst to Malcolm but that was one of her favorite songs around the house when she was growing up. She held onto every note that floated out of his mouth. She was mesmerized by how effortlessly he was belting out the notes and how poised he was about it.

Zaddy Issues

By the time he was approaching the end of the song her nipples were tingling and her clit was throbbing. She couldn't excuse herself in the middle of the song just to go wipe herself up. That would have not only been rude but kind of obvious considering she had just been to use the restroom less than ten minutes before switching rooms. So, she stood there marinating in her own juices while Malcolm's singing produced a continuous flow.

"So, what do you think now? Can I…play?" Malcolm sarcastically asked. The tone of his voice and his choice of words were the ultimate double entendre. She wanted to take it and run with it just to see how far it would go. But again, she thought of how she could possibly be misreading what she thought may have been signals. It wasn't worth risking the opportunity of a lifetime. Whether it was the effects of the honey or her unbridled attraction to his debonair persona, she was way beyond turned on. He could tell that she was really into his performance by the way she was leaning across the front of the piano swaying her hips from side to side even after the playing stopped. "Oh yeah…you can…play" she responded. Malcolm smiled then began to play again. He sang and played "If This World Were Mine" by Luther Vandross then "A Ribbon In The Sky" by Stevie Wonder. The more he played the further in Ebonee leaned towards him captivated by his renditions of each classic hit. By the time he finished his Stevie piece Ebonee was in full blown lust mode. "Have you ever played before" Malcolm asked. Still floating in her own little world his question caught her off guard. "Huh? Umm no! I used to want to learn until my father said I'd have to be taught by the lady at his church. She was so mean to everyone except for me" she answered. Malcolm looked confused and asked, "If she was mean to everyone except you, then why wouldn't you do it?" She stood upright with one hand on her hip and said, "The only reason she wasn't mean to me is because she was thirsting for my daddy, and I wasn't having it." Malcolm burst out laughing at how she was pouting as if she was still a child in church. He stopped laughing then patted the piano bench and said "Well what if I…taught you a few things? Would you be willing to learn from me?" Her heart skipped a beat then started racing until went into overdrive. She wanted to jump across that piano and let him have his way with her. It was the second double entendre he threw at her. Throwing caution in the wind she responded with "It depends on what kind of things you want to teach me. I'm not a little girl anymore." Malcolm stroked his beard and said, "Come find out."

Zaddy Issues

Ebonee sauntered her way around to the front of the piano with her index finger slowly dragging along the edge of the instrument. She took her seat next to Malcolm and said "I guess we're switching roles. Now you're the teacher and I guess I'm the student now." She bit down on her bottom lip then scooted in even closer to Malcolm until their faces were only inches away from touching. "I'm here. Teach me!" she said lightly. He slowly leaned in and placed his lips on hers. Ebonee opened her mouth and allowed Malcolm's tongue to enter. The rich taste of Malcolm's expensive wine coated both of their tongues. Their hands and arms wrapped around each other groping and squeezing like two mating octopi. Their long-awaited passionate kiss was a relief to Ebonee. She sat back and asked "Is this the lesson? If so, I already knew how to kiss. Although you are a damn good kisser, I was expecting a little higher learning than that." Pleasantly shocked at Ebonee's boldness, Malcolm was more than willing to give her everything that she was asking for. "Oh really? So, you're going to be one of those sassy kind of students huh? Well, that wasn't your lesson. That was your placement test before you start to learn" he said with a grin. Ebonee giggled and asked, "You mean like in college when they test you to see what level classes to start you on?" Malcolm nodded his head with an even bigger grin and told

Zaddy Issues

her "Exactly! You've heard of the school of hard knocks? Well, this is the school of hard Cox. So how about forgetting about a higher learning and get a...deeper education? Have a seat in my lap and let me show you some strokes" he ordered. She liked the fact that he was being cool enough to be receptive to her little role play vibe. "Ok...ok. I can do that" she said as she stood up to get in position. As soon as she was directly in front of Malcolm, he gently placed his hands around her waist and stopped her from taking her seat. She looked back over her shoulder at Malcolm and asked "What are you doing? I thought you said to sit in your lap." He turned her around to look at her face to face. He looked into her eyes with less of a grin but a more authoritative look on his face and said "I told you. This is 'deeper' learning. Take off your pants!" The sensually commanding undertone in his voice was arousing to her. She wasn't wasting any time to snatch her oversized sweatpants off. Malcolm grabbed her hands and said "Stop. There's no rush. Take your time. I have cars than can go from zero to sixty in a matter of seconds. But I don't drive them that fast. Do you know why?" Almost childlike Ebonee shook her head "no". Malcolm slowly relaxed his grip until he was holding just the tips of her fingers. He looked up at her and said "Babygirl just because it can go that fast doesn't mean it should always go that fast.

Zaddy Issues

More often than not, you get more pleasure out of it when you start off slowly cruising on the city streets showing off the magnificence in the design of its body. But once you've gotten it all heated up from cruising, that's when you are going need to feed a little speed to it. Then you can jump on the highway and get low with it."

Amazed and convinced by the logic of his analogy Ebonee began to slowly undress. She started with her sweatshirt. Patiently Malcolm gazed upon her golden tone flesh as she eased the shirt upward. Just as the garment was covering her face to clear her head Malcolm pulled her to him by her bare waist. Gently he placed his open mouth next to her exposed stomach. His tongue moved from the top of her naval up to the bottom of her bra. With her eyes blindfolded by the sweatshirt and hands entangled in the sleeves still, she was vulnerable to his every advance. Malcolm found no need to waste time with unfastening the clasp in the front of her bra. In one swift snatch the clasp was destroyed and Ebonee's large perky breasts popped out bouncing around like a Jack in the box. She took in a deep breath when she felt his hands corralling her lively breasts. They fit inside of his hands as though they were made for each other. Again, his tongue became active repeatedly racing from one nipple to the next. She could barely stand still. Her hips and cheeks banged against the keys of the piano with every shift and shuffle. She freed herself from the shirt and damaged bra when she felt Malcolm's hands and attention move to the waistband of her pants. He eased them down past her wide hips until she was able to wiggle them enough to free fall to the floor. She stepped out of shoes and pants then stood before him in nothing but her satin panties. Malcolm slid the piano bench back for more space then unfastened his belt and jeans displaying a pinned down erection that stretched from the center of his jeans to the far side of his front pocket. Ebonee's eyes grew twice their size at the sight of how long and thick he was looking inside of his jeans. "Now turn and face the piano" he ordered. Without a word she slowly turned as he requested. Once she was in place Malcolm placed his hands on her hips then pulled her panties to her feet. "Now, have a seat. It's time to learn" Malcolm said softly. She eased herself down until she felt the thick tip of his dick head brush against tingling clit. Her thick legs quivered from what felt like never ending inches entering her moist swollen walls. She leaned back against him and discovered that he had removed his shirt as well. She pressed her back against well defined chest and gripped the edges of the bench once he was balls deep inside of her. She could feel him deep inside of her. It felt as though he was shifting her cervix. With every

Zaddy Issues

circular grind of her hips that Ebonee gave, Malcolm was there to receive and return in perfect synchronization. Ebonee reached back behind Malcolm and held on to his smooth bald head while she enjoyed the ride. Her mouth flew open, and moans of pleasure poured out from the touches of Malcolm's hands caressing her hard nipples.

Her lesson continued when Malcolm pulled her down behind her then interlocked his arms with hers. Then the lesson escalated when he forced them both to their feet with Malcolm still deep inside of her. Ebonee's moans echoed beyond the large piano room to throughout the house. "YES...YES...YESSSS! Right there!" she cried out from feeling Malcolm stretching her open with his slow methodical grind. Up and around his hips moved pushing himself deeper and deeper forcing her wetness to pour out all over him. He scooped and twirled around in and out of her until Ebonee could hardly stand it. Suddenly he released her arms then placed his left hand at the base of her neck. "Spread your legs a little and grab your ankles!" he demanded with his hand firmly sliding down her back and nudging her downward. Malcolm's hands held onto Ebonee's fluffy soft hips like handlebars on a bike. The long deep strokes came slowly and repeatedly until Malcolm announced, "Remember what I said about taking a nice car out to cruise?" Ebonee looked up at Malcolm with her hair hanging over her head and slowly bouncing from his rhythmically smooth thrusts. "Mmmmm yeeees. I like cruuuising with youuuu" she moaned. "That's good. I'm glad you like it" he responded. "But we're about to hit the onramp to the highway. You might want to buckle up and hold on" he added as his thrusts gradually grew from a slow wind to pure dick pounding. He was hitting every spot and corner that she was aching for Trevor to reach. Her ass cheeks bounced and rippled from the thrashing it was receiving. "FUCK!" she cried. "If you say so…" Malcolm responded as if her outcry was a request. Nevertheless, he shifted gears on her and switched from a rapid pounding to slamming her body into his dick until she began to yell out "You're gonna make me cum…you're gonna make…meeeee…OH SHIT! YEEES YEEES YEEEEEES!" Her knees and thighs began to tremble and shake sporadically from the pressure she was feeling inside building up.

Just when she thought she was about to explode all over him Malcolm quickly sat back down onto the piano bench pulling Ebonee with him. When he did that, his shaft shot even deeper inside until she could feel him nearly touching her stomach from the inside. "FUCK" she yelled out again. As before Malcolm responded. "Don't mind if I do" he said just

Zaddy Issues

before he reached down and grabbed both of Ebonee's legs. He pulled them both upward forcing her hips slightly forward to open her for the straight shot of dick Malcolm began to throw in her hard and fast. The way she was positioned had the thick wide vein on the back of his rock-hard dick gliding back and forth against her g-spot better than any of her silicone toys at home. They all felt good but none of them could do what Malcolm was doing. They couldn't whisper in her ear the way he was doing. "Are you still liking your lesson?" he whispered. "Yes" she answered in a light tone. "Yes what?" he asked. "Yes...I like it" again she answered. He lowered her legs so that she could place her feet firmly on the floor while he continued to grind inside of her. Then he advised "When you were in school and your teacher asked you a question, you said 'yes sir or no sir'. Did you not?" Feeling him rolling around deep inside of her walls along with the sound of his deep voice rumbling in her ear made her cream even more. "Yeees" again she moaned. That's when Malcolm took to his feet again taking Ebonee with him still engaged. He bent Ebonee over and grabbed her by the shoulders then rapidly power drove his dick into her until his balls were bouncing off of her clit like a punching bag. "In...my...class... you... say... yes sir!" He was fucking her so hard and fast that she had to reach out and grab the front of the piano to keep from being thrown into it. "YES SIR! YEEES SIR…SIR…SIRRRRR" she screamed out as she came all over Malcolm. Over and over, he plunged inside of her with his hands firmly gripping her soft shoulders. "You're about to get your first grade. Are you ready for it?" he asked breathing heavily. "Yes sir. Yes sir. Give it to me" Ebonee begged. Malcolm's deep voice roared out aloud as he pulled out and shot his cum across her back and ass. Load after load he sprayed his semen in the air like a gushing geyser splashing everywhere.

Chapter 13

About Last Night

The next morning Ebonee woke up groggy and disheveled as usual but in an enormous bed that she knew wasn't her own. She looked around the large room and immediately remembered that she had gotten too sleepy to drive home. Malcolm demanded that she stay the night. Then she noticed that he was no longer in the bed but a note instead. It read "I hope you don't mind that I left. I had some business to tend to early today. You were sleeping so peacefully that I didn't want to wake you. Feel free to make yourself at home and help yourself to whatever you'd like. You are more than welcome to stay as long as you want. Also, I left a towel, wash cloth and new toothbrush in the master bathroom so that you can freshen up. I should be back there just before nightfall. However, if you have to leave, I understand. But if you do, I would love for you to come back later. There are instructions to the alarm system on the kitchen table if you do leave and a spare key next to the instructions if you choose to come back. FYI: I'm hoping that you will be there when I return. I have a surprise for you. Sincerely Malcolm." She was so excited that she threw herself back into the bed smiling from ear to ear with her legs kicking in the air. She couldn't wait to tell the girls. She rushed downstairs to find her phone still in the kitchen. She picked it up to quickly call the girls and saw that she had multiple missed calls and several unanswered text messages from Trevor. She had forgotten that she was supposed to call him when she got back from Malcolm's so that they could plan their date for that night. She was caught between a rock and a hard place. She wanted to see Malcolm again, but she didn't want to back out on Trevor either. She needed a plan and fast.

She reached out to the one person that she felt that she could count on in a clutch like this, her girl Nicole. Nicole told her to use the oldest trick in the book. After having her consultative call with Nicole, she gathered her things and rushed home. On her way she called Trevor to break the bad news about not feeling too well due to starting her fictitious menstrual cycle. Any man would appreciate a heads up with that. As expected, he didn't have any issues with accepting a rain check considering the misperceived situation. After running home to grab a "spend the night" bag and shower, she stopped by the restaurant to make sure everything was running smoothly without her being there for the day. Before heading back to Malcolm's, she stopped by the grocery store to grab some things for dinner. She wanted to be able to cook

Zaddy Issues

a nice meal for Malcolm without any distractions. That way she could possibly get another lesson early. She was finishing up the meal when she heard a car pull into the driveway. Moments later the front door opened and closed. The sound of Malcolm's heel walking across the marble floors echoed down the hallway growing louder and louder the closer he got to the kitchen. He stepped into the kitchen and Ebonee's knees buckled. His slim fitting custom made suit was hanging on him as if he was born for it. The snug fitting slacks created a noticeable imprint running down his left thigh that gave grey sweatpants a run for the money. "I'm really glad to see that you're still here. Something smells delicious. What is it?" Malcolm asked as he walked up to Ebonee for a hug and kiss. The mere touch of his lips nearly threw Ebonee into a fit. "Ummm…huh? Oh yeah. I grabbed some lamb chops and things from the store earlier. Just a little something for tonight. I hope you like it" she struggled to explain. He stroked his beard and answered "Are you kidding me? I love lamb." Malcolm walked over to the stove to spy on what Ebonee had going on. She followed behind him then wrapped her arms around his waist from behind and said "I'm about to fix our plates. No stealing out of the pot…sir!" Pleased to see that she was still embracing the "sir" energy from the night before, Malcolm turned to face her and said "No problem. I can wait. Besides, as much as I love lamb, I'm just as excited to see what you have for dessert." He gave her a kiss on the forehead then started walking away saying "I'm going to go wash up. I'm starved." Ebonee leaned against the counter rubbing her thighs together as she watched him walk off.

After dinner they sat at the table and talked over a bottle of wine. "I've been invited to a private gala next week. It's a plus one event. Would you mind accompanying me and be my plus one?" Malcolm asked pulling a pair of tickets from his vest pocket. Ebonee's eyes lit up. "I've never been to a gala. Sure, I'd love to go. When next week?" she asked looking at the tickets. "Wait...does that say Anthony Hamilton on those tickets?" she questioned snatching the tickets from Malcolm's hand. He fell out laughing and said "Yes. He's going to be the guest performer for the evening. It's actually in just a few days from now. It's this Wednesday coming up. Are you good with that?" Ebonee was speechless for a moment with her mouth wide open. She jumped out of her seat and straight into Malcolm's lap. She wrapped her arms around his neck and said "I own my own business too...sir! I make my own schedule. Wednesday is fine. That gives me just enough time to go shopping for something to wear." Then she stood up to clear the dinner plates from the

Zaddy Issues

table. On her way to the sink Malcolm's phone buzzed notifying him of a text message. After reading the message he got up and walked over to Ebonee. He placed his hands on her hips and said, "You don't have to do that." She giggled and said "I don't mind. It's only a couple of plates and forks. I'm almost done already." He turned her around and said with a laugh "No silly. Not the dishes. I mean shopping. That was my tailor on the phone. He just arrived in town and will be here tomorrow to fit you for your gown. I hope that you don't mind that I was a bit presumptuous. But he came in from Chicago to fit me for my tux and I wanted to be prepared just in case you said yes. There wouldn't have been enough time for him to come back. So, I told him to bring a couple of options for you to choose from when he came. That way all he has to do is go back to Chicago and work his magic on whatever you choose. He can have us set in no time." Once again, she was left speechless with her mouth open. Everything was feeling like a dream. She wanted to call the girls so bad that she didn't know what to do. "Well ok then. I was hoping that you didn't think that 'I' was being too presumptuous by bringing an overnight bag. But I guess it's a good thing that I did seeing that I need to be here tomorrow anyway in order to get fitted. Huh?" she teased. Malcolm wrapped his arms around her

Zaddy Issues

waist and said "Looks like it worked out for both of us. I'm going to run upstairs to come out of this suit and get a little more comfortable while you finish up down here." They kissed and he was off to head upstairs.

Malcolm was finishing his shower when he heard the bedroom door open and close. "I'm almost done. I just need to rinse off and I'll be…" he was saying when the foggy glass shower door crept open. There stood Ebonee as bare as the day she entered the world. With soap still rolling down most of his body Ebonee told him "No need to rush. Let me help you get clean? Then maybe you can help me get to some of those hard-to-reach places from the back?" He wiped the soap and water from his face and beard to get a clearer view of her nudeness. She stepped inside of the oversized shower with three showerheads spraying from the ceiling aimed at the center where they stood. Ebonee walked up to Malcolm's opened arms and accepted with watery embrace. She placed her head on his dripping wet chest and gave him a kiss in the middle of his chest. Hot shower water shot from the ceiling onto the top of Malcolm's bald head and cascaded down his glistening dark body. Water rushed from his beard onto her cleavage. She left hand and began to wipe away the excess soap from his body while her right hand worked on clearing any soap from his noticeable iron stiff erection. Gradually

Zaddy Issues

her kisses made their way downward from his chest to the top of his stomach until she was in a full squat slurping on the head of his dick. Even with both hands stroking him her mouth was still full. Deep throating was out of the question, but she was willing to stuff as much of him in her mouth as she possibly could. Sucking and twisting with both hands-on Malcolm at the same time was driving him insane. He placed both hands on the back of her head and slowly fucked her pretty mouth. "Yeeees. Suck it!" he moaned in pleasure. He was so deep in her throat that she could feel the tip of his dick passing her back teeth. She could taste the precum leaking onto her tongue every time she would squeeze down on him with her mouth. "Gawk gawk gawk gawk…" echoed amidst the sound of water beating on the tile in the shower. On the brink of exploding in Ebonee's mouth Malcolm told her "Stand up and face the wall!" She slowly dragged the long hard piece of meat from between her wet mouth and said, "Yes sir." She arched her back then rose up onto her tip toes with her hands spreading her watery wet cheeks open for Malcolm to slide in. once he was inside of her, like an assailant about to get frisked, Ebonee assumed the position in the corner with her hands firmly placed on the adjacent walls. Ebonee clawed at the slippery tiled shower walls as Malcolm repeatedly slid in and out of hers. His hands cupped and gripped her glistening breasts from behind. She could feel his balls smacking her from behind sloshing water around between her legs. The deeper her went the stronger the sensation to cum filled her body until she could stand it anymore. The yearning feeling to cum overcame her as she released a shower of her own all over Malcolm's stabbing pole.

After a night of extraordinary sex Ebonee thought that it couldn't get any better until she woke up with Malcolm face first between her thighs having her for breakfast. "Good morning beautiful" he announced when she raised her head. "Mmmm good morning" she moaned. "I hope you don't mind that I helped myself" he suggested. Before she could respond, Malcolm's phone began to ring. He jumped up to grab his phone. "Good morning" he said. "No, it's not too early at all. I'm actually already up and having a little breakfast. Did you get enough sleep?" he said to the caller. "No problem. We will be ready by the time you get here. See you soon" he stated before ending the call. "As much as I would love to continue, we should probably finish this another time. Pierre will be here soon. Plus, I have some real breakfast food downstairs waiting on us" he advised. "I'll see you downstairs. Hurry before your food gets cold" he said before walking out of the room to head downstairs. On the way down the stairs her nose was greeted by the aroma of hotcakes, sausage and eggs lingering along the staircase. When Ebonee finally made it to the kitchen she was shocked to find another woman with her back turned fixing plates. Not only that but she was about the same age as Ebonee and was beautiful. Ebonee stopped short of entering the kitchen to glance over at Malcolm who was face first into his newspaper. She stepped in and cleared her throat to announce her presence. "Ummm good morning" she said in the direction of the other woman. The woman turned with a plate of food in each hand and happily responded back "Good morning. You're just in time." Malcolm folded his newspaper then uncrossed his legs and said "Ahhh there you are. Ebonee I'd like you to meet Monica. Monica comes over from time to time to make sure that I have a well-balanced meal. She also works for me. She's a big part of the reason why I get to everywhere that I need to be. Without her I'd be in a world of trouble" he explained. Ebonee did all that she could to muster up a smile and asked Monica "Where's your plate? Aren't you going to join us?" Monica sat the two plates on the table then turned to Ebonee and smiled. "Oh, I've already…had a filling breakfast" she responded. Then Monica leaned in and gave Malcolm a kiss on the cheek. "I'm going to get out of you all's hair and let you

Zaddy Issues

enjoy…your breakfasts" Monica explained giving Ebonee the up and down once over with her eyes as she walked past Ebonee on her way out of the kitchen. Monica stopped at the entranceway of the kitchen then looked back at Malcolm and said "Call me if you need me. You know where I'll be." She smiled at Ebonee before walking out and said "It was nice meeting you. I sure hope to see more of you around here." Ebonee took her seat at the table then looked at Malcolm and asked, "What does she mean 'she's already had a filling breakfast'? I don't see her plate anywhere." Malcolm reached out and placed his hand on Ebonee's knee and asked, "Are you jealous?" Ebonee crossed her leg to remove Malcolm's hand. "No. I'm not jealous. I just…you know? She seemed mighty…excited that's all" she lied. "Don't pay her any mind. She's harmless. Now eat up. Pierre will be here soon, and we need to be ready when he gets here." Malcolm suggested with a conformational smile.

Chapter 14

The Web We Weave

After spending an afternoon getting fitted and measured by Malcolm's tailor Pierre, Ebonee prepared a quick lunch for them before heading back to her own home. On the drive home she received a call from Trevor. "Hey you" she answered. "Well, hello. I've been calling you. I was about ready to send the folks to come on you" Trevor answered with concern mixed with half of a chuckle. "Yeeeah, I know. I'm sorry but I've been experiencing some pretty unusually abnormal cramping that's had me feeling horrible. I've been taking medicine that has had me knocked out. I didn't even go into the restaurant yesterday. I spent the entire day and night at home in bed" she added. "Humph really? Because I went by the restaurant to surprise you and Candace said you came in but left early. So, I went by your place to check on you when I tried calling and didn't get an answer, but your car wasn't there" Trevor questioned. "Yeah well, I took my car to the shop to have some work done after leaving the restaurant. The shop gave me a ride back home. So that's why you didn't see my car. I just picked it up this morning" she responded compiling the list of her lies she started.

Zaddy Issues

"Wait...you came to my house without asking first? Look I appreciate the concern and all but please don't do that again" she demanded. "Say less. I didn't mean to overstep any boundaries. I was just trying to be considerate. But don't worry. It won't happen again" he snapped. For a moment there was an awkward silence between the two that quickly ended when Trevor said, "How about you give me a call when you're off of your cycle and not so moody." Then he hung up before she could even respond. The phone call left her with mixed emotions. On one hand she felt guilty about all of the lying to Trevor. She really liked everything about him with the exception of what he was lacking in the bedroom. Then on the other hand she didn't like the fact that he assumed it was okay to pop up at her house unannounced. It was something she had always thought to be the signs of a stalker. After dealing with Malcolm's overly zealous assistant and the phone call with Trevor, she couldn't wait to get home to get a glass of wine to settle her nerves.

In her rush to get home the sound of a siren drowned out the music from her radio. Switching from the fast lane of the highway she realized the police car switched lanes with her. As if this day couldn't get any worse for her it found a way to do just that. She pulled over on the highway and the police car pulled up right behind her with lights and siren still

Zaddy Issues

blaring behind her. Knowing the first thing the officer was going to ask for was her license, registration and proof of insurance she grabbed her registration from her glove box. She was in a deep dive into her oversized purse searching for her insurance card when the officer approached her window. At first all she saw from waist to chest was the black uniform and belt with a gun attached. She rolled down her window and asked, "May I ask why you're stopping me?" Ebonee was prepared to flash a little cleavage and use her womanly wilds to get out of a ticket if necessary. But the voice of a female officer put that notion to rest real fast. "You were going seventy-eight miles per hour in a fifty-five. What's the rush?" the officer responded. Surprised at the realization that it was not only a female officer speaking but a black female officer at that, Ebonee tore her attention away from her purse. "I was rushing home because I remembered that I left some food on the stove cooking. I was just running to the store to get a couple of things. I just live two exits away officer. Can I please go before my stove catches on fire?" Ebonee nervously answered. The officer glanced around in the car then back at Ebonee. "I don't see any grocery bags in the car?" the officer said. Thinking quick Ebonee responded "I never made it to the store. I remembered the food and turned around. That's why I was speeding officer." The officer smirked and said "I tell you what. Let me get your license and registration so I can run it real quick. If you don't have any warrants or outstanding tickets, then I'll let you go. Sit tight. This shouldn't take long." Ebonee watched the officer in her side mirror as she walked back to her cruiser. Ebonee sat patiently in her car praying that the officer would keep her word because she needed that drink of wine even more than ever. She glanced up into her rearview mirror and spotted the officer sitting in her cruiser looking back at her. She smiled at the officer and the officer smiled back then got out of her car to head back to Ebonee. On her way back to speak to Ebonee she stopped halfway to respond to a call coming in on her radio attached to her shoulder. Ebonee couldn't really hear what was being said but she could tell from the look on the officer's face that it must've been something serious. All of a sudden, the officer rushed up and double tapped the trunk of Ebonee's car then yelled "Ms. Lawrence you can go. Just slow down!" Then the officer turned and ran back to her car in a mad dash. She jumped inside and sped off in a hurry with lights and siren on full blast.

Later that evening Ebonee was sitting on her couch reading a book and working on her third glass of wine when she received a knock at her front door. She had already spoken

Zaddy Issues

with Gina and Nicole, so she knew it wasn't one of them and she wasn't expecting any other company. "I know damn well Trevor didn't bring his ass back to my house uninvited again after I just told him not to do that again" she thought to herself. She rushed to the door stomping with her game face on. She was going to give Trevor a piece of her mind without him being able to hang up on her this time. She had just enough wine to get her out of character. "WHO IS IT?" she barked at the door. "It's the police ma'am. Open up!" the voice on the other side answered. She quickly slammed her hands against the door then peeped through the peephole and froze stiff. It wasn't just any officer. It was the female cop that pulled her over earlier in the day. Except for she wasn't in her uniform this time. Instead of her uniform she was wearing a pair of shiny black skintight leggings, a shear black and white polka dot top with a black bra showing through. Her hair and makeup were flawless. She looked nothing like Ebonee remembered from earlier. Ebonee opened the door with her jaw dropped. "Wooow look at you officer. How did you find me?" Ebonee said smiling. "I got your address from your license, which I failed to give back before I got called away. Instead of having your things mailed to you I wanted to save you the time of having to wait for the mail. So, I brought them to you myself when my shift ended" she explained to Ebonee. "Well, that was really kind of you officerrrr…" Ebonee responded probing to get a name. "Mitchell…Officer Mitchell. But you can call me Melanie" she responded with her hand extended with Ebonee's paperwork and license in it. Ebonee accepted the things and asked "Where are my manners? Would you like to come inside? I was just about to open up another bottle of wine." Melanie smiled and said "Maybe some other time. I'm actually about to head uptown to meet up with some of my girls. We have a seven thirty reservation at Uptown Cuisine. I hear it's pretty nice…expensive as hell but nice. I'd hate to be late. It's hard to get in. Have you ever been?" Ebonee giggled and said "Oh yeah! I've been plenty of times. As a matter of fact, I'm there damn near every day." Melanie's eyes squinted and her head tilted to the side. "Really? I guess you must really like it then huh?" Melanie asked. Ebonee laughed and said, "Yeah, I guess you could even say 'I love it'. I'm the owner of Uptown Cuisine." Melanie covered her mouth with her hand and said "Shut…up! Oh my God! Really?" Ebonee began to blush and said "Yeah really. As a matter of fact, as a token of my appreciation for letting me slide earlier, dinner for you and your girls is on the house tonight. Give me one second and let me grab one of my business cards." She left Melanie

Zaddy Issues

standing in the doorway stunned while she ran off to her bedroom to get her card.

When Ebonee returned Melanie was still standing with her hand over her mouth. "Here you go. When you get there give there ask for Candace. I'm going to give her a call to let her know to take good care of you ladies. My cell phone number is on the card. Give me a call some time when you can come have a little wine with me like you said. I'd love to hear some of your police stories. I'm sure you have some good ones." Ebonee said as she handed Melanie her business card. Melanie took the card and said "Oh absolutely. You don't have to threaten me with a good time. As a matter of fact, I'll bring the wine. You'll be hearing from me soon." Ebonee gave Melanie smile and said "I better. I'm holding you to it." Melanie nodded her head and said "What about this weekend? I'm free Saturday if you are." With the way she and Trevor ended their last call she knew she wouldn't be seeing him anytime soon if ever and no plans to see Malcolm. She answered "Cool. Why not? It's a date. You bring the wine and I'll cook dinner. Is seven good for you?" Melanie happily responded before walking off "Seven is perfect. I'll be here." Melanie thanked Ebonee again before heading back to her car. Ebonee stood in the door and admired Melanie's jiggling cheeks as she walked off.

Chapter 15

It Must Be Nice

Wednesday morning Ebonee woke up to a text from Malcolm. "Good morning gorgeous. Your dress for tonight is ready and waiting for your beautiful body. Send me your address and I can have William to come pick you up if you'd like so that you don't have to leave your car at the airport. We need to be there by noon. It's a three-hour flight." She had to rub her eyes to make sure that she was reading the text correctly. Instead of responding to Malcolm's text, Ebonee felt this was more worthy of a call. He picked up on the first ring. "I knew you would call" he said. "What is this talk about leaving my car at an airport?" Ebonee asked fighting back her enthusiasm. She didn't want to lose her cool over the phone like some high school freshman asked out by the senior quarterback. "I thought the dinner was here in Charlotte. Why do we need to go to the airport?" she continued. "Babygirl the gala is in Chicago. I thought you saw that on the tickets" he said laughing. His laughter came to a halt when he realized that he was the only one laughing. "Wait, is that a problem?" he asked not knowing that Ebonee was on the other end doing her best happy dance in the

Zaddy Issues

middle of her bed. She plopped down on the bed with her legs folded so that she could gather herself enough to respond. She took a deep breath then held the phone away from her face to clear her throat and said "Well I hadn't planned to go to Chicago tonight, but I don't see why not. When were you planning to come back to Charlotte?" Malcolm let out a big sigh of relief and said "You almost made me pass out. For a second there I thought you were going to say that you couldn't go." Malcolm took a moment to get himself together and continued "I have a nine o'clock meeting back here tomorrow morning. So, we'll be back no later than seven. Plus, it'll be Thursday and I have another class on Thursday." Ebonee laughed and said "Now hold on there, teacher's pet. We said every other Tuesday and Thursday. You just had a lesson last week. Besides, I'm used to teaching students that bring a regular size number two pencil to class. You're in class writing with one of those thick kindergartner pencils. That thing's not a standard number two. That's more like a number ten with extra heavy lead. Your next cooking lesson isn't until Tuesday...sir!" she teased. "That's all well and good. But I was talking about MY class. Oh, and William is about to head out to run an errand before coming to get you. Now please, send me your address and get ready. He can be there in a couple of hours" he said. Ebonee's heart started racing with excitement. "Yes sir" she said softly then got off of the phone to do what was asked of her.

When William arrived Ebonee headed out with a small rolling suitcase. "You're not going to need that" William said standing by the opened car door. Ebonee stopped at the car and said, "It has my makeup and a change of clothes and a few things that I might need while I'm away." The old tall gentleman laughed and said "Trust me. Where you're going, Mr. Cox has someone to do your makeup for you and everything you'll need. All you have to do darling is show up." Then he took her bag and placed it in the trunk while Ebonee got in the backseat. William got in the driver's seat and tuned the radio station to a smooth jazz station. They drove through the neighborhood and jumped on the highway. William glanced into the rearview mirror and noticed Ebonee bobbing her head to the music. "They don't make music like this anymore" he said. "That's because there will never be another Duke Ellington. The master" she responded. William's eye darted back into the mirror. "What do you know about 'The Duke'? He was way before your time" he asked in his raspy old voice. "My mother was a big Duke fan. Gospel music and Duke Ellington is what we listened to every Saturday morning while cleaning the house

Zaddy Issues

when I was growing up. I had no choice. Eventually I loved him too" she said gazing out of the window smiling. "I see why he likes you so" William mumbled. "Excuse me" Ebonee questioned. "I said he really likes you; you know. He talks about you all of the time. I've been driving for him for over fifteen years now and I've never seen him this way over a woman since the Mrs. But I see it now. I like you too. You're different" William elaborated. "Awwww that's so sweet. Thank you Mr. William I like you guys too" she emotionally expressed. He smiled then looked back into the mirror at Ebonee and said "Thanks darling. And because I do like you, I want to give you a heads up. His daughter Ashley can be quite the piece of work. And that's me being respectful. She really loves her dad but ever since her mother passed, she's been really overprotective of her father. Because of that he never takes any of his women around her either. She can be extremely rude and nasty. She means well, I guess. But I get the feeling you can probably hold your own." Ebonee was still trying to process her newly acquired information when William announced "We're almost there. I trust that I can count on you to keep our little conversation between the two of us…right?" Ebonee reached across the seat and patted William on the shoulder and said, "It'll be our little secret Mr. William." He reached back and placed his hand on top of hers then said "Thank you sweetie. And please, call me William."

They turned off of the main street then down a long strip of road until they pulled up to a building with several private jets behind it. William grabs his cell phone as they pulled around the side of the building. "Mr. Cox we're here about to pull around to you now" he said before hanging up. They pulled into a hanger with two private jets inside with Malcolm standing between the two wearing a long black trench coat and black fedora with a pair of black gloves in his hands. In her mind it was like something out of a scene from a gangster movie. Malcolm opened Ebonee's car door when they pulled up to him. He removed his hat and gave her a kiss as soon as she stepped out of the car. "Ready to get some wind beneath your wings" Malcolm jokingly asked. Waving her finger back and forth at the two planes Ebonee smiled from ear to ear and said "Absolutely. Are we going in one of these planes?" Malcolm laughed at her antics and said "No baby. The plane we're taking is about to pull up any second." Ebonee nodded her head up and down saying "Oooh gotcha. I was wondering why we needed such a big plane unless we were taking half of Charlotte with us. They're like commercial planes huh?" again Malcolm smiled then said "No they're not commercial. They're mine

Zaddy Issues

too." Ebonee's jaw dropped and both hands flew straight up to cover her mouth. Before she could even catch her breath good, the roaring sound of a plane filled the opened hanger. "That's the plane we're taking" Malcolm shouted over the noise from the engine of their plane pulling up just outside of the hanger. Ebonee slowly turned around to the opening of the hanger to see a plane big enough to place either of the other two inside off it. She turned to Malcolm and gave him a playful punch in the shoulder and asked "Why are we taking the biggest of the three if it's just us? Either one of these would be more than enough room for just us." Malcolm patted twice on the roof of the car and William pulled off. "We're taking this one because it's faster. And it also has a bigger bed" Malcolm said to Ebonee while grabbing her hand to walk her to the plane.

Chapter 16

Welcome To The Mile High Club

They approached the onboard ladder to the plane where a tall beautiful dark skinned female attendant awaited them. She greeted them with a smile saying "Good afternoon, sir...ma'am. The crew is prepared for takeoff whenever you are." They walked up the stairs and into the doorway where they were greeted by three more ladies just as beautiful as the first. One of the ladies was dressed in a flight attendant's uniform like the first one. But the other two were wearing pilot uniforms. "Let me take your coats?" the attendant suggested. They took off their coats while Malcolm introduced the crew to Ebonee. "Thank you, Olivia. Ebonee, Olivia here is one of the two attendants joining us on the trip. And you met Joya outside" he said pointing back at Joya walking up the steps to board the plane. Olivia and Joya smiled and shook Ebonee's hand then exited to prepare for takeoff. "And these are our pilot and copilot, Captain Tasia and Co-Pilot Morgan. They will be in charge of getting us to and from Chicago safely" Malcolm confidently advised. Ebonee shook hands with both pilots them followed Malcolm towards the back of the plane to take a seat. Ebonee

Zaddy Issues

was amazed at the inside of the plane. She never imagined shiny hardwood flooring in a plane that matched the wood grained interior. There were two plush white leather seats facing the front of the plane with an identical seat on the opposite side back-to-back. Another set of four were positioned in the same manner only a couple of feet away. "This is where we will sit when we take off and land or if the pilot instructs us to" Malcolm explained patting on one of the large seats as he walked past it to continue giving Ebonee a tour of the vessel. Once they passed the seats, they walked through a doorway that led to the middle area of the plane furnished with a large white leather sectional setting along the walls of the plane. Two round cocktail tables with four swivel chairs at each were bolted down in the center of the room. A small well stocked bar with two bar stools sat at the back of the area just before the entranceway to the sleeping quarters. Malcolm stopped between the two tables and waved his hand out then said, "And this is where we relax and chill after takeoff." He stepped through the doorway of the sleeping quarters and held his hand out for Ebonee to follow him inside. She grabbed his hand and joined him. Malcolm closed the sliding door behind her turned to the elaborate king size bed then said, "And in here…is where I teaccch!" He placed his hands on the sides of her face then

Zaddy Issues

gave her a kiss. "And it's soundproofed too. Once this door is closed, they can't hear us, and we can't hear them without using the intercom system" he added. Ebonee wrapped her arms around Malcolm's neck and said, "Is that right?" She looked over her shoulder at the closed door then back at Malcolm and said "Well we will see about that. I might have to put those doors to the test." Malcolm grinned then gave her another kiss and said "Yeah that's right. And so is the door between the takeoff area and the sitting area.

They took their seats up front and prepared themselves for takeoff. Once in the air Joya walked up to Malcolm and Ebonee to make an announcement. "Today's lunch is lobster roll and macaroni salad paired with a 2001 vintage German Riesling that I think you will find rather exquisite. I'll bring your plates to the sitting area whenever your ready sir" Joya happily advised before walking back to the sitting area. Ebonee leaned over to Malcolm and said "I don't know about you, but I haven't eaten all day. I'm starved and I love seafood." Malcolm laughed then stood and jokingly responded "And I love a good German Riesling." They headed into to sitting area to find Olivia standing behind the bar pouring two glasses of wine for them while Joya prepared their plates on the opposite side of the plane. They took a seat at the table closest to the sleeping quarters for the

Zaddy Issues

best view out of elongated window over the sectional. Olivia walked over with their drinks and sat them down then asked Malcolm "Would you care to have a smoke when you're done with lunch sir?" Malcolm looked across the table at Ebonee and asked, "Would you mind if I smoked?" The look of shock on Ebonee's face instantly drew concern. "I don't have to smoke. It's fine" Malcolm quickly explained. Ebonee burst out laughing and said "No it's not a problem. I just never imagined you smoking a cigarette. That's all." Malcolm laughed with her and said "That's good because I don't smoke cigarettes. She was talking about cannabis. See when I first started flying private, I used to be a nervous wreck. Olivia saw how bad off I was offered a little of what she had for the flight back. I was so relaxed on the flight back that I invested in a cannabis company in Florida. Ever since then I made sure that I had some of the best available whenever I flew. But I'm at the point now that I don't have anxiety about flying now. Now it's just more like a ritual. But like I said...I don't have to smoke if it will bother you in any way." Ebonee scrunched up her face and said "Child please! I used to be a big pot head back in college. I haven't smoked in years, but I might even take a toke with you. I don't mind." Malcolm smiled and tilted his head at Ebonee then looked up at Olivia. He gave her a nod then off she went and up walked Joya with their food.

After eating they moved over to the sectional to get more comfortable. Once they were settled in Joya walked up with a small silver tray in her hand and sat it on the table in front of them. On the tray was a silver lighter, a silver ashtray and two pre-rolled joints. Olivia followed up and topped off their wine glasses then sat the remainder of the bottle next to the silver tray. The two of them stood in front of Malcolm and Ebonee. "Will you need anything else sir?" Olivia asked. "No that will be all. Thank you, ladies!" he responded. They walked off together to the takeoff area and closed the door behind themselves. Malcolm set fire to one of the joints from the tray then deeply inhaled. He sat back with a mouth full of smoke and stretched his arms across the back of the sectional with Ebonee snuggly nestled under his left. He took a couple of more tokes before passing it to her. "You might want to take it slow if you haven't smoked in awhile. This isn't your average street corner smoke. This is the good shit" he warned. She took a toke then burst into an uncontrollable coughing spell and quickly handed it back to Malcolm. She took a gulp of her wine to ease the stinging sensation in the back of her throat and said "You weren't lying. I know it's been a while but DAMN! That is TOO strong. I'm on cloud nine already." Malcolm took a couple of more hits then sat the joint in the ashtray then said "Now you know how I feel when you're around. You make me feel like I'm on a cloud when we're together. I feel like a young man again when I'm with you. I hope you don't mind me saying this, but I've been with multiple women since losing my wife. But none of them were able to make me feel the way you do. I haven't felt this alive since Hollie passed. You make me feel happy again." He leaned in and gave her a kiss guiding her to lie back on the cushion of the sectional. Malcolm slid to the floor on his knees never losing connection of their deeply enthralled kiss. Together they worked frantically to remove her formfitting jeans and panties. She kicked off both shoes sending them to free fall across the airplane.

Ebonee sat up to assist Malcolm with pulling her shirt off over her head. Malcolm remained on his knees positioned between her legs. He grabbed her by the hips then snatched her towards his face. Ebonee's hands flew back behind her head to grab the back of the soft leather of her seat from the touch of Malcolm's initial stroke of his tongue meeting her tingling clit and wet pussy lips. Malcolm's plump lips surrounded her lady flower like a warm blanket of love. The more he worked his massive lips around the wetter she became. Reaching around her legs to grab the inside of her thighs his hands spread her open even more for his tongue to dive deep into her. With his tongue darting in and out of her and his lips locked around her love entrance drawing it in like a vacuum, Ebonee began to lather his beard with her own natural balm. She looked down at the crown of his shiny bald head and couldn't resist from reaching out to pull it closer to her. The slickness of his smooth head in her hands made her walls ache for more. Around and around, she rolled her hips thrusting herself against his bearded face slowly bouncing off of her. "Mmmm yeeees" she repeatedly moaned. Her sounds of pleasure drove Malcolm to engage even more. Licking her like she was his last meal had Ebonee's juices pouring from her by the mouthfuls. She had been tongue fucked plenty of times in the past but not like that. No one had ever taken their time and made her feel like it wasn't a chore. It didn't feel as though he was just trying to get her wet. It wasn't a bunch of aimless lapping like some thirsty puppy. Not only was he slow and gentle but there was genuine passion and sensitivity. Her breaking point was when his full attention aimed for the top of her clit with the back of his tongue. Back and forth it gently brushed around. Her walls began to contract, and her legs began to tremble. She could feel the flow of her juices starting to build up inside of herself. "Don't stop" she begged. Obediently he

Zaddy Issues

continued his oral lashing while Ebonee repeatedly slammed his face into her squirting hole. "I'M CUUUUMING!" she yelled to the top of her voice. Malcolm's beard was drenched with the evidence of her confessions. "Ok everyone! This is your Co-Pilot Morgan. We're about fifteen to twenty minutes from landing. Attendants and passengers prepare for landing. I will announce when everyone needs to be in their seats and buckled momentarily. Thank you for the opportunity to pilot you today" rang out over the intercom system just as Ebonee was climaxing. "At least we got to finish this time" Malcolm said with a smile and wiping his beard.

Chapter 17

Guess Who's Coming To Dinner

When they landed in Chicago Malcolm had a car and driver waiting for them at another private airstrip. Ebonee couldn't help for noticing that his driver was also a young beautiful black female. She drove them from the airstrip to a beautiful home right outside of the city. They walked up to the door and Malcolm entered the security code to unlock the door for them. While taking off their coats to hang on a coat tree, the sound of footsteps drew closer towards them. "Ahhh you're here. Welcome back home sir." Pierre announced as he appeared from around a corner to greet them. He gave Malcolm a firm handshake and embraced Ebonee with a hug. "It's good to see you as well Ms. Ebonee. The make-up girl and the rest of the ladies are waiting for you. If you don't mind following me, I will take you to them" he said as he turned to head back around the corner. He stopped short of his turn then looked back at Malcolm and said "Oh and sir I have your ensemble in the master bedroom upstairs when you're ready. Also, Ashley called and said she wouldn't be able to make it tonight. However, she will be in Charlotte next week to discuss the wedding plans." Malcolm's facial

Zaddy Issues

expression was full of disappointment. "What is it this time?" he asked in a brisk tone. "Well, she was rather vague with me. And somewhat difficult to say the least. I think it may have something to do with her fiancé...Kenny. But don't worry yourself with that now. You go upstairs and relax while I get Ms. Ebonee taken care of. I'll have a glass of scotch sent to your room momentarily." Pierre suggested in his usual snobbish and unbothered demeanor. Malcolm nodded his head in agreement with Pierre and stood with his hands in his pockets watching Ebonee and Pierre walk away. Pierre escorted Ebonee to her makeover crew and returned her three hours later to Malcolm looking like royalty. When Ebonee and Pierre rejoined Malcolm, they met him standing at the front door in a stunningly stylish black tuxedo with a small gift bag in his hand. "Well look at you! You clean up very nicely young man" Ebonee joked putting her arms around Malcolm's neck. Pierre gave a loud clutching single clap and said smiling "Looks like my job is done here. I'm going to retire early with a glass or two see what I can find on Hulu. You know how to reach me if you need me for anything. You two have a wonderful time and I will see you the next time you're in town. Ms. Ebonee, I enjoyed spending the day with you. And I would be remiss if I left without telling you again how marvelous that red looks on you.

Zaddy Issues

Absolutely marvelous. Muah!" He grabbed his hat and coat then left pleased with his handy work. "We need to get going too. But before we leave, I have something for you" Malcolm said handing Ebonee the bag he was holding. She reached inside and pulled out a small thin box. She took one look and turned beet red in the face. "And what do you want me to do with this...sir?" she blushingly asked. "Well sometimes these dinners can become somewhat eh...boring. They start out nice, but I've been to enough of them to know that at the end of the day, it's really just a bunch of people with more money than sense trying to outdo one another. I figured we'd spice it up a little when thing started to become less entertaining. What do you say? I mean unless you don't think you can handle it...then you know. I get it." Malcolm explained with a sneaky little grin. Ebonee flicked her wrist around with the box in her hand pretending to have an attitude. "Man PLEASE! I have plenty of toys at home. Trust me when I tell you, I can handle some little vibrating panties with no problem" she bragged before prancing off to the bathroom to change. Malcolm snapped his fingers in the air twice and said "Ummm let me get that remote from in the box before you go Ms. Bad Ass." She turned and said "Ooooh. I see how you want to play now. Ok ok you can have the remote. I'm still not scared." She dug inside of the

Zaddy Issues

box and tossed the small remote to him and said, "Just know that you better not start something that you can't finish, or we'll be either leaving early." Malcolm laughed then rushed off to find batteries.

Chapter 18

Dinner With A Buzz

They spent the first hour with Malcolm introducing Ebonee to multiple wealthy black people that the average American had no idea about their existence let alone that there was even such another world. A world where black people dressed, talked and acted like uppity white people. It didn't take long for Ebonee to see what Malcolm was talking about back at the house. Even being the owner of a five-star restaurant of her own, she had never seen so many fake people with so much money in one place. For whatever personal reasons, several of the men present were attempting to rub elbows with the handful of white people that were there. But in Malcolm's case it was just the other way around. Every white person in the elaborate ballroom eventually made it their duty to not just speak with Malcolm but to go out of their way to make their way to their table to speak to him. When the entertainment began everyone took their seats at their tables to listen to the soulful sounds of Anthony Hamilton. He sang some of his old songs as well as a couple of his latest hits. At the end of his set one hundred plus guests erupted in a roar of applause. Ebonee was standing with the

Zaddy Issues

rest of the audience for his standing ovation when all of a sudden, her knees buckled from the buzzing vibration between her thighs caused by the panties Malcolm gave her to wear. Shocked and caught off guard her hand instinctively clutched her midsection. When she looked over at Malcolm, he was staring at her with a devilish grin. He held up the tiny remote up in his hand mostly concealed and gave her a little wave. The other two couples sitting at the table with them were obviously unaware of the remote fornication that was going right in front of them. When the applause stopped so did the vibrating. Everyone sat back down and Malcolm and Ebonee never lost eye contact. Ebonee gave Malcolm a smirk and a nod as if to say, "you got me but I'm still good." Throughout the rest of the night Malcolm would tap the remote button periodically trying to catch Ebonee off guard. He kept the remote tucked away in his pants pocket for easy access. He had even gotten to where he no longer had to put his hand inside of his pocket. He could feel the button he needed through the fabric of his pants. His best jolt of vibration was when he caught Ebonee just as she was taking a sip of her drink and nearly spat champagne all over a city councilman while having a conversation. She had to play off the sudden body jerk as though she was fake sneezing. By the end of the night her panties were drenched thanks to Malcolm and his lustful mischief.

Malcolm and Ebonee were on the dance floor slow dancing to the smooth sounds of Maxwell's song 'Til The Cops Come Knockin' when Malcolm whispered in Ebonee's ear "What do you say to us avoiding the crowd leaving and the awkward empty promises to keep in touch? And let's get out of here before everyone else." She smiled and said, "I'd like that." Like thieves in the night, they exited the dance floor and slid out of the crowded ballroom without anyone noticing. They walked through the lavish lobby and up to the concierge counter. "Welcome back to The Ritz-Carlton, Chicago Mr. Cox. It's been a while. Are you enjoying your time here?" the man behind the counter said. "Well, if you call spending an evening with a ballroom full of vampires enjoyable, I would say no. But if you call spending the evening listening to one of my favorite singers perform live while sitting with the most beautiful woman in the room enjoyable then I would say absolutely." Malcolm explained while gazing into Ebonee's eyes. "I'd have to agree. I saw the guests and if you don't mind me saying sir, you definitely had the best…view in the event" the man suggested. "Thank you, Adam. I don't mind at all. I'm quite lucky to have such eye candy on my arm" Malcolm responded with his eyes still

Zaddy Issues

locked in on Ebonee's eyes and her blushing eyes were locked in on his as well. "Splendid sir! Will you be needing any assistance with any bags this evening?" Adam asked. "Not tonight. We'll be leaving before sunup. We just need a little rest before an early flight in the morning" Malcolm said turning his attention back to Adam. "Well, here is your keycard sir. I assume an escort won't be necessary either." Adam said as he slid the keycard across the countertop to Malcolm. Malcolm took the card and said, "You assumed right my friend." Then Ebonee and Malcolm walked away to catch the penthouse elevator. They rode the elevator to the thirty fifth floor to a penthouse that could easily be featured on "The Lifestyles of The Rich and Famous". "Welcome to my little humble abode. Make yourself at home" Malcolm said unraveling his bowtie then taking off his tuxedo jacket. "The master suite is down the hall. You can shower and freshen up there as well. I just need to make a few calls to check on things back home and with my daughter. I'll be back there when I'm done" he continued as he walked off towards the balcony. "If this is what you call a humble abode then I'd like to see what you consider luxurious" she said looking around in amazement. "What am I supposed to wear tomorrow? I don't have any of my clothes I packed" Ebonee questioned. Malcolm stopped and turned back around and

Zaddy Issues

said "Oh don't worry. I already had clothes bought and brought here for you. You have a closet full of clothes, shoes, underwear and anything else that you need. And don't worry I got your sizes the first night we spent together." He gave her a wink and a smile then turned back around to head to the balcony with his phone up to his ear. That was the most thoughtful thing any man had ever done for her. She pranced to the back of the penthouse to look for the master suite so that she could freshen up while Malcolm made his calls.

Ebonee unexpectedly finished her shower alone. She walked back up front wearing just a plush white robe to find Malcolm still on the balcony talking on the phone. From the way he was pacing around with his hand flailing it was obvious that the conversation wasn't going well. Ebonee didn't want to interrupt so she quietly took a seat on the couch with her feet curled behind her watching Malcolm give someone the business over the phone. It was the first time she had seen him so serious since the altercation at her restaurant with the unruly customer. When Malcolm noticed that Ebonee was watching him he ended his call then walked back inside. He took a seat next to Ebonee and said "I apologize. I didn't mean to stay on the phone for so long. I missed the shower." She reached behind Malcolm to stroke the back of his head. "It's fine. Is everything okay back home?" she asked sensing the tension in Malcolm. Forcing himself to smile he answered "Yeah, everything is fine. Or at least they will be if I could just get my thick-skulled daughter of mine to listen to me sometimes. But she's so head over hills for some loser. She barely knows the piece of shit and he has her so wide open that she can't even see that he's just using her. But she's thirty-two years old. I can't force her to stay away from him like she's some child. You know? But I just hate to see her get hurt and I know it's coming." Even through his fake smile Ebonee could feel the pain in his heart. It was the same look that she received from her father when she brought her college boyfriend Charles home on what was supposed to be a weekend visit until Charles got caught smoking weed behind the house. Her father had never been so upset with her. Ebonee sat up then pulled him into her arms and placed his head on her shoulder. She wanted to be able to offer some words of advice but how could she when she was practically the same age as his daughter. "I'm sorry. I didn't mean to ruin the mood" Malcolm sadly confessed. Ebonee caressed the side of his face and told him "Nonsense. You haven't ruined a thing." Malcolm laid his head in her lap and stretched out across the couch. "Thank you. I'm glad you're here with me. It gets lonely sometimes" Malcolm continued to pour out. "You don't have to thank

Zaddy Issues

me. I thank you! Thank you for allowing me into your world and for opening up to me this way" she said rubbing on his shoulder.

Chapter 19

No Means No

The next day at work Ebonee received multiple calls from Trevor. She let them all go to voicemail without returning any of them. At least until she received his text saying, "I guess you're still on your cycle huh?" That was the last straw for her. She decided enough was enough. She wasn't about to let some short dick many with more muscles than manners talk to her that way and get away with it. She called him immediately after reading his rude text. "I knew that would get you on the phone. Why didn't you answer any of my calls before I had to be an asshole?" Trevor said when he answered the call. "I find it hard to believe that you weren't an asshole before you sent that childish text. You really surprised me. I gave you more credit than that. I was busy WOOORKING while you were constantly blowing up my damn phone like some teenager. But then again, I shouldn't be surprised at this type of behavior coming from a man than doesn't know that it's not okay to pop up at someone's house without calling first or being invited. What grown ass man does that? Ebonee lashed out. Embarrassed and ashamed Trevor barked back "The kind of man that you let blow your back out the first time you invite him to your home. That kind!" Amused at Trevor's level of confidence Ebonee laughed out and said "Boy PLEASE! I've had sneezes that were longer than that sample size dick of yours. You would have come out better using one of them strong ass fingers of yours. Maybe then you would have been able to reach my spot." Trevor attempted to make a comeback comment but was hung up on before he could get a word out. He called back immediately and was sent to voicemail. His second attempt to callback got his number blocked.

Later that night Ebonee called up the girls to tell them all about Trevor. "See that's why you can't trust these little dick men. You give him an inch and he doesn't know what to do because he's not used to having inches" Nicole joked on their call. "So does this mean you're dating Mr. Rogers now?" Gina asked sarcastically. "Please…Mr. Rogers wish he had it going on like Zaddy Malcolm. He flew our girl to Chicago on his private jet. Mr. Rogers ain't got shit but that little toy train rolling around in his little make-believe town. Just stop it already" Nicole said before Ebonee could respond for herself. "Look, I'm not dating anyone right now. Malcolm and I are just enjoying the moment. Besides, after trying the dating thing with Trevor I'm not sure that I even want a commitment anymore. At least not right now

Zaddy Issues

anyway" Ebonee explained. "Look there's nothing wrong with having a little fun. All I'm saying is that you can have fun with someone closer to your age. That's all. Besides, what if you accidently end up pregnant by this old ass man? He might mess around and die on you and then what? I'll tell you what. You'll be stuck raising a baby by yourself. That's what" Gina debated. "On that crazy ass note, I'm getting off the phone. Ebonee girl, don't listen to Old Mother Hubbard's ass. There's nothing wrong with an older man. And from the sounds of it, if he dies then you and your baby would be rich. I'm gone" Nicole announced just before hanging up. "Yeah, you're really reaching. I'm out too. Goodnight sis" Ebonee said before hanging up also. Ebonee sat on her couch after getting off of the phone and thought about all of that had transpired within the past few days. Not wanting to give too much thought in Trevor she turned on the television to catch the local evening news before bed. The news anchor was finishing up a report on a string of deadly attacks on African American women around the city. The following story was about deadly car wreck on highway 77 involving a BMW i7 and a tractor trailer truck. Ebonee frantically grabbed her phone and called Malcolm. She tried multiple times and his phone just kept going to voicemail.

Chapter 20

What In The World Is Going On

The news eventually confirmed that the deadly crash was in fact Malcolm's car that was involved. He survived the crash but unfortunately William did not. Days went by and Ebonee still hadn't heard anything from Malcolm. It wasn't until late that Friday night just before going to bed that she finally received the phone call that she had been waiting to receive. It was Malcolm. Frantically she answered "Hello...hello! Malcolm?" Her heart raced waiting for a response. In a fragile tone he answered, "Good evening babygirl." Her heart skipped a beat when she heard dhow weak, he sounded. "Oh my God! Are you okay? How do you feel? What hospital are you in? Can you have visitors? I'm getting dressed! I'm coming to see you! You poor thing! Where are you?" Ebonee ranted without even letting him answer the first question before bombarding him with more. "I'm fine. The doctor said I should be able to go home Sunday or Monday. I wish that you could come but the visiting hours are over for the day. I have a couple of bruised ribs and a concussion. So, the doctor wants me to stay through the weekend so that they can keep an eye on me until I'm cleared

Zaddy Issues

from this concussion. It's nothing major. I'm just really tired and sore. Plus, they have me on some kind of pain killer that is kicking my ass. That's why I wanted to call you before I passed out sleeping again. But...but...William. He...he..." Malcolm struggled to say before bursting into tears. Ebonee's heart was crushed at the sound of pain and tears. Helplessly she began to weep with him. "I know. I heard on the news. He was such a sweet man. My condolences and prayers go out to you and his family. I'm so sorry that you are hurting. I wish that I could be there to give you a hug" she expressed through her teary voice. Malcolm gathered his composure and said "Thank you babygirl. That means the world to me. He wasn't just my driver. He was my best friend Eddie's father. I hired him not because he needed the job. He was a retired bank president with literally nothing else to do with his spare time. Money was the least of his worries. My friend passed away years ago from lung cancer and his mother died before he was a teenager. William never remarried and pretty much raised Eddie by himself. After Eddie passed William retired and was bored. He reached out to me one day when he saw me in town visiting my father. We had lunch together one day and the next thing I knew he was back in New York with me. He said driving for me was his way of holding on to a piece of Eddie. He loved being

Zaddy Issues

back in Charlotte. He would always reminisce about when he coached Eddie and me in little league baseball. My parents loved him too. He was a great man. Now he's back with his wife and Eddie. I'm going to miss him dearly." Malcolm's heartfelt story struck Ebonee's heart to the core. "Fuck it! I'm on my way. They're going to let me inside! Damn the visiting hours! What hospital are you in?" she passionately declared with conviction. She jumped out of her bed looking for something to quickly throw on while still waiting for Malcolm to reveal his location. Straining from laughing Malcolm said "Wait. It's okay. I'm really sleepy and you're way too pretty to go to jail. They'll eat you up in there. You can come first thing in the morning. I'm not going anywhere. I promise. And I'm not telling you which hospital I'm in until I talk to you again in the morning. So, get you some rest and I'm going to do the same. I will see you in the morning. Okay?" Ebonee pouted and said "Are you sure? Cause I don't mind coming tonight and in the morning. And I'm NOT going to jail. And if I do my girls will have me out in time to see you in the morning. And I PROMISE you THAT!" He wincingly laughed and said "I'm sure they would. But really, I'm fine. Just let me get a little rest so that I can have some energy and I'll see you tomorrow." Ebonee pouted a bit but reluctantly agreed to wait until the morning.

Zaddy Issues

Early the next morning Ebonee woke up from her restless sleep to her phone's text notification. It was from Malcolm with his location and room number. She wasted no time getting cute. She threw on a pair of jeans, sweatshirt and sneakers then rolled out. When she got to his room there was a nurse and Malcolm's daughter Ashley. Ebonee recognized her from seeing her at the restaurant with Malcolm. Ashley was looking out of the window and talking on the phone with her back turned when Ebonee walked in. Malcolm was sitting on the edge of the bed with the nurse was finishing up taking his vital signs. The nurse was heading out of the room when Malcolm spotted Ebonee. "Heeeey babygirl" he said with a glow. Ebonee tossed her purse in an empty chair and rushed to his side to give him a big hug. Ashley turned to see what was going on then quickly got off of the phone. She gave Ebonee a glare and asked "Ummm excuse me but who are you?" Ebonee released her embrace and extended her hand to Ashley to shake and said "Oh I'm sorry. My name is Ebonee. I'm a friend of Malcolm." Ashley looked down at Ebonee's hand then looked Ebonee up and down with a frown and said, "You're a bit young to be calling my father by his first name aren't you...Ebonee?" Ashley walked over to the other side of Malcolm's bed and folded her arms refusing to shake Ebonee's hand. "Stop it! Just stop it!

Zaddy Issues

Ebonee is my friend, and I won't have you speaking to her that way." Malcolm said scolding Ashley. "Ooooh, I see! This must be one of your newbies huh? And where did you find this one daddy? From the looks of her I'd say Amazon Prime." Ashley sarcastically snarled with laughter. "EXCUSE ME! I'm no one's newbie. You don't know me or anything about me. And I suggest you watch your mouth before you find out!" Ebonee fired back. "Wait…I remember you. You're the one that owns that little restaurant downtown. Yeeeah, I remember now. So, what, you're on his team now? It's all coming together now. He needed a cook and who better to add to the stable than another young thing" Ashley said adding more fuel to her fire. Ebonee started to walk around to the other side of the bed when Malcolm jumped up and grabbed her arm. He turned to Ashley and said "Now damn it that's enough. Ebonee is who I have hired to do some work for me AND to cater your wedding with that sorry ass so called man of yours. If you can't show some respect, then I suggest you leave." Ashley grabbed her purse off of his bed and threw it on her shoulder then headed for the door staring at Ebonee on her way. She stopped at the entrance and said "I'm leaving only because I have things to do. But before I go Eeeeebonee. I'm going to tell you like I've told the others. I don't know what you think you might

Zaddy Issues

get out of my father but whatever it is you can forget it. I've seen your kind before. And I don't care who you are or what he says. You're just another notch in his belt. So don't fool yourself. You're eventually going in the stable with the rest of them." Then she turned around and walked away.

Ebonee turned to Malcolm and asked, "What in the hell just happened?" It was clear that Malcolm was embarrassed. They took a seat together on the edge of his bed. Malcolm hung his head then looked back at Ebonee and said "I apologize for her behavior. She wasn't always that nasty. After her mom passed, she never accepted the fact that I started dating again. It wasn't easy for me either to be honest. But when I did start back, I realized that I didn't want to be in another monogamous relationship. I didn't want to hide it from Ashley, so I told her." Ebonee jumped up and said "Wait. What do you mean you didn't want to be monogamous? So, what, are you some kind of wannabe pimp or something? Is that what she meant by adding me to some stable? Because I'm not here for that. I need some answers." Malcolm jumped to his feet also and said "wait…" but doubled over from the pain in his ribs before he could say anything else. Ebonee instinctively reached out to help him have a seat back on the bed. Still doubled over Malcolm grimaced to catch his breath. Struggling to breath he said

Zaddy Issues

"Let me explain. It's not like that." As he was lying back in the bed to finish explaining there was a knock at the door. Without an invitation the room door slowly crept open. Ebonee looked over her shoulder to find none other than Monica walking through the door. "Hiiiii! Oh my gosh. How are you feeling? You poor baby!" Monica said trotting over to Malcolm and brushing past Ebonee as if she wasn't there. She hugged Malcolm then gave him a kiss on top of his head. Then she finally looked back at Ebonee and said "Thank you for coming to check on him. He's so lucky to have women like us on his team. I knew when I saw you that morning that you were a keeper." Ebonee was furious. She looked at Monica then rolled her eyes and said "Team? Oh no baby. I'm not on any TEAM. I play solo!" Ebonee snatched up her purse and stomped out. She could hear Malcolm's failed attempts to yell for her to come back. Hurt and feeling betrayed she ran down the halls of the hospital in tears.

Chapter 21

Something Different

Ebonee spent the rest of the day at home alone drowning her sorrows in ice cream and cookies. She wanted to call the girls but just wasn't up for hearing Gina's mouth about dealing with an older man. Nor was she up for Nicole suggesting to go shoot up the place. It was far less stressful to just sit and watch Lifetime movies than to deal with everything else. Midway through her third movie her phone buzzed. Assuming it may have been another call from Malcolm she started to ignore it. But judging from the short buzz she knew that it wasn't a call but a text instead. She still thought to ignore it thinking it may had been from one of the girls she still checked it anyway. It was from none of the expected. It was a text from Melanie. "Hey you! Just checking to see if we were still on for tomorrow night" the text read. Ebonee had almost completely forgotten about her girl date with Officer Mitchell. "Are you kidding me? With the kind of week, I've had since I saw you, I need a little girl on girl time. I hope you have more than one bottle to bring. I'm going to need it. You might even need to bring your handcuffs just in case I get a little disorderly." Ebonee texted back with three

Zaddy Issues

laughing emojis with tears at the end of the message. "Say less. I'll see you tomorrow night with plenty for you" Melanie responded with three heart emojis at the end of her response. Ebonee responded with a smiley emoji with hearts for eyes to show her approval. A few minutes went by without a text. Just as Ebonee was getting back into her movie the phone buzzed again. "I might need to bring my night stick too huh?" She knew then that Officer Mitchell wanted more than come share cop stories. Ebonee responded "That might not be a bad idea. I can get a little unruly when I have too much wine. I may have to be forcefully detained." Ebonee hadn't been with another woman since college but at that moment she was experiencing some old familiar desires that she hadn't felt since back then. Maybe it was the fact that Melanie was so tall and beautiful that turned her on but whatever it was, she had Ebonee's attention. Melanie ended with "Luckily for me that I have the proper tools and training to handle such situations. I'll see you tomorrow night. Be ready to assume the position. Or else I may have to use force." Ebonee responded with water emojis and "See you tomorrow night…officer."

That next night Ebonee was in the kitchen finishing up the dinner she prepared for her and Melanie when she heard a familiar knock at her door. She trotted from the kitchen to

Zaddy Issues

answer the door. Ebonee opened the door for Melanie and jokingly said "You do know you don't have to knock like you're still on the clock, right?" Melanie laughed then held up two bottles of wine and said "My bad! Force of habit. But at least I have wiiiine." Ebonee laughed back and said "In that case, come on in officer. And I'll take those and put them in the refrigerator so they can start chilling." Ebonee took the bottles then gave them a look and said "Ooooh this is that Earl Stevens by E-40. I've heard about this, but I haven't tried any yet. Is it pretty good? I heard it was strong too." Melanie sat her purse in the recliner and took a seat on the couch while Ebonee was heading towards the kitchen. "Yeah, it's pretty good to me. And you heard right. It's pretty strong. I hope you like it" Melanie responded. Ebonee peeped her head from around the corner of the kitchen wall back at Melanie and said "Girl please. If its wine…I like it!" Then she disappeared back around the corner. "Dinner should be ready shortly. Meanwhile I have a bottle of wine that I started on the other night. We can finish it off until the other two are ready" Ebonee explained as she reappeared from the kitchen with two glasses of wine for them to get started on. She took a seat next to Melanie then handed her a glass and said "So you're a Steelers I see. Are you originally from Pittsburgh?" Melanie glanced down at the football jersey she was wearing and said "No I'm originally from Miami. I just threw on something comfortable and relaxed. But my father is a big Steelers fan. So are my two older brothers. I didn't have much of a choice in the matter." Ebonee laughed and said "Girl the way you looked poured into those jeans I can't tell you're comfortable. But I can relate. My father is a Carolina Panthers fan. Every Sunday during football season he would watch the games and I would come sit with him pretending that I liked it. But I just liked hanging out with him. It was hilarious seeing him cut up over the game. Eventually I started enjoying the game myself. Before I knew it, I was a big Panthers fan too." Melanie nodded her head understanding Ebonee's explanation all too well. Ebonee took a sip from her glass then gazed at Melanie and added "In fact, between that fine as coach Tomlin and how good you look in that jersey ya'll bout to make me jump ship." Melanie smiled and said "Thank you. And you've never lied. Mike Tomlin is one fine black MAN! I'd play a little two hand touch with him any day. Hell, he could even tackle me."

After dinner they sat and talked about everything under the sun. Ebonee shared her story from growing up a preacher's kid to how she became the owner of Uptown Cuisine. She even told her all about her recent relationships with Darrius,

Zaddy Issues

Trevor and Malcolm. In return Melanie talked about how following her father and brothers' footsteps led to her working in law enforcement. She also shared her story of being recruited by multiple WNBA teams before a knee injury in college ended her career. But the cop stories as she promised was the highlight for Ebonee. During the stories Ebonee clung to her words the way she did whenever Malcolm would speak. "Wow. You're the only police officer that I actually know and had in my house. And I've damn sure never gotten drunk with one before. And I am definitely feeling this, Earl Stevens. This shit ain't no JOKE!" Ebonee cackled. Melanie grabbed the bottle of wine and divided the remainder between their two glasses. When she sat the bottle down, she said "Yeah this has eighteen percent alcohol in it. This isn't for light weights. Besides, you said you had a rough past few days, so I brought out the big guns for you. It's not too much for you, is it?" Ebonee sat up in her seat to look Melanie in the eyes. She said "I know cops are supposed to be known for being able to handle their alcohol. But so, can I. I am…a big girl you know?" Melanie chuckled at Ebonee and asked, "Is that right?" Ebonee's eyes bucked open then said "I may not be as tall as you but yes. I'm very much so a big girl." Ebonee stood up and put her hands on her hips then slowly spun all the way around saying, "You

Zaddy Issues

better recognize." She was making her second spin with her hands in the air when Melanie gave Ebonee a tap on the ass. Her cheek bounced around in her snug fitting cut off sweatpants. Ebonee stopped then looked back over her shoulder at Melanie and said, "Umm I believe that's police brutality ma'am." She finished her spin then plopped down on the couch and fell back into the plush cushion of her seat. "Oh no boo. That was far from brutality. Like I said...I'm from Miami baby. I was just trying to see what you were twerking with back there" Melanie explained with a sneaky grin.

Although Ebonee was never known for her dance skills, she could hold her own with basic steps. Ebonee sat up in her seat giving Melanie a blank stare with her mouth open. "I know damn well you saw all this ass back there" Ebonee questioned. Melanie sat back in her seat then crossed her legs and started staring back at Ebonee. Melanie locked her fingers together and placed her hands on her knees then lowered to almost a squint. "Oh, I saw it and it's nice and soft too. But the question is, do you know how to move 'all that ass. Or is it just for show?" Melanie inquired then took a bite of her bottom lip as if she was trying to taste herself. Ebonee stood up for the challenge. "Oh, you don't think I can twerk?" Ebonee asked with her hands on her hips.

Zaddy Issues

Melanie extended her hand towards the open space in the room and said, "Let's see what you have then short stack." Ebonee stepped to the center of the floor and turned to face Melanie. "You ready?" Ebonee asked. Melanie nodded to give her the go ahead. Ebonee turned around then placed her hands on her knees and began to do her best version of twerking. Her cheeks repeatedly bounced and clapped rapidly with force. She looked back at Ebonee's unbothered facial expression then got down on all four attempting to draw some kind of emotion from Melanie. She began to bounce even harder. Eventually Melanie stood up and said, "Sweetie get your drunk ass up before you hurt yourself." She extended her hand to help Ebonee to her feet. "Girl please! You know I was killing it" Ebonee insisted breathing heavily with a smile and straightening out her clothes. "If you say so boo. If you say so…" Melanie expressed as she unnecessarily assisted Ebonee back to her seat. Ebonee looked up at Melanie and said, "And I guess you can do better?"

Melanie grabbed her phone from the coffee table and asked Ebonee "Do you have a speaker that I can connect to my phone?" Ebonee's eyes bucked then she said "Oh you want music? Okay hand me your phone. I'll connect it to my surround sound system." Ebonee connected the phone then

Zaddy Issues

gave it back to her. Melanie tapped on the screen a few times then started playing one of her favorite songs, "WAP" by Cardi B and Megan Thee Stallion. When the beat dropped Melanie sat her phone down and said, "Pay attention and take notes!" Melanie started bobbing her head and bouncing to the intro beat. "There some hoes in this house!" the intro repeated. Cardi B started her verse and Melanie went straight into action. She began twirling her perfectly round ass in a circle hypnotizing Ebonee. She started off slowly then gradually sped up while she was also dropping into a squatting position at the same time. Her hips were jerking and bouncing perfectly to the beat. By the time Megan's verse kicked in Melanie was on all fours crawling towards Ebonee's opened thighs. She stopped just before getting within Ebonee's reach. She quickly dipped down and arched her back with her face on the carpet then stretched her arms out then started grinding to the beat. Ebonee was so aroused that she didn't even realize that she had slipped her hand inside of her panties until she felt the moisture between her lips. She quickly snatched her hand out just before Melanie had looked back up. Ebonee neared came on herself when Melanie ended the song with a full split alternating bouncing her cheeks. Melanie jumped to her feet when she was done and asked "What do you think now? Was that better?"

Zaddy Issues

Ebonee grinned and jokingly said "It was aight. You had a whole routine didn't ya? Let me find out you be on the pole at The Phat Khat Club when you're not arresting people." Melanie took a seat next to Ebonee and laughed. "You couldn't pay me enough money to even take a hat off in that funky ass place. Now if you would have said The Showroom, you might have been on to something" Melanie teased. Melanie grabbed her glass of wine and took a sip then burst out laughing at the look of shock on Ebonee's face. "I'm joking silly. Actually, my ex-wife and I took a few strip tease classes awhile back attempting to spice up our failing marriage. She got the house, and I got the dance moves." Melanie nonchalantly explained. Ebonee knew that Melanie was feeling her, and she was definitely feeling Melanie as well, but she wasn't expecting to hear that she was once married to another woman. "OH! I had no idea you were…" Ebonee started saying before Melanie interrupted. "What…divorced? Because I know you weren't about to say that you didn't know that I liked women when you and I both have been eye fucking each other from the day I came here to return your things" Melanie interjected. Ebonee was at a loss for words. Melanie was spot on, but Ebonee was not expecting her to be so upfront nor as expressive.

Zaddy Issues

"Actually, I was going to say that I had no idea that you were married before. What happened?" Ebonee said. Melanie sat her glass down and said "Well she couldn't handle my job. I got promoted to detective and that's when things started to spiral. I don't hold any hard feelings towards her though. I get it. Being a cop's wife isn't any easier than being a cop. And being a detective's wife is even harder." Ebonee looked confused and asked "Wait…if you're a detective then why were you driving a police cruiser in full uniform writing tickets?" Melanie nodded her head up and down a few times then said "Look at you picking up clues and shit. We might need to get you on the team. Good catch. But I was picking up some extra hours for the holidays. It was the only kind of overtime available at the time. But since this recent string of murders, I can put my uniform back in the closet. This case is giving all of us plenty of work trying to catch whoever it is." Ebonee's eyes lit up. "I remember seeing something on the news the other night about that, but I didn't hear the entire story. I hope you all catch whoever it is too. But just make sure you're careful out there. Hell, maybe you SHOULD be working at The Showroom. It damn sure has to be less risky" Ebonee exclaimed with concern. Then she began to look at Melanie as though she was the candy that her sweet tooth was craving. "I'd pay to see you" Ebonee

Zaddy Issues

suggested in a coy voice. Melanie smiled and asked, "Is that right?" Ebonee subconsciously began to rub her thighs together and answered "Mmmm hmm but not with you wearing those jeans of course." Melanie downed the remainder of wine in her glass and said "Oh Boo you don't have to go to The Showroom nor pay. Your pretty ass can get it for free tonight."

Chapter 22

Lunch Is On You

They made their way to the bedroom for Melanie's private performance for Ebonee. Ebonee took a seat in her favorite book reading chair while Melanie stood in front of her. "Oh wait…I almost forgot. Wait right here and don't move. I'll be right back" Melanie demanded before walking back out of the bedroom. Ebonee sat patiently while she could hear Melanie in the living room moving around. "Is everything okay?" Ebonee yelled into the living room. She was about to get up to check on Melanie when out of nowhere she heard music starting to play. She paused and sat back in the chair when she saw Melanie step into the doorway wearing nothing but her football jersey and twirling a pair of handcuffs around her index finger. Melanie's hand sprung upward to grab the side of the door frame as if she was trying to spread it open wider at the same time the lyrics dropped. Usher's song began playing throughout the house. "It's seven o'clock on the dot. I'm in my drop top…cruising the streets…" started as Melanie began to slowly wind her hips to the beat. Melanie sauntered towards Ebonee in a seductively rhythmic stroll tossing the handcuffs onto the

Zaddy Issues

bed. Melanie gave Ebonee a lap dance performance that would have rivaled even the best stripper on the east coast. The song and dance ended with Melanie sitting in Ebonee's lap with her back pressed firmly against Ebonee's large breasts. Melanie held her head back then placed her lips against Ebonee's and was not denied. After their passionate kiss Melanie stood up and walked over to the bed. Slowly she crawled on allowing her jersey to rise up enough to display Melanie's tattooed buttocks and lower back. Ebonee sat up and said "That is too cute. I'm guessing the red M&M character on the left cheek is for Melanie and the yellow one is for Mitchell. And with the ampersand sign at the top of that sexy little ass just brings them together huh? I see what you did there. Cute…real cute." Melanie looked back over her shoulder and responded "But unlike the candy, I melt in your mouth, and I'll nut…in your hand. I told you. You have an eye for clues. You sure you don't want to try out for the force. I know people. I could get you in if you play your cards right. And by cards, I mean me. I'm the cards" Melanie teased then rolled over onto her back with her legs opened and twirling her handcuffs waiting for Ebonee to accept her invitation to her candy.

That next morning Ebonee woke up and rolled over to an empty bed and a buzzing cell phone. She looked around the room for Melanie and she was nowhere in sight. She called out for her and nothing. Ebonee got up and checked the living room to find that Melanie and all of her things were gone. The sudden buzz of the phone in her hand prompted her to check her notifications. She had a text message from Melanie but what stood out the most were the numerous missed calls, voicemail messages and multiple text messages all from Malcolm. Still miffed with Malcolm she ignored his notifications and all of the other unimportant requests for attention to jump straight to Melanie's. The text read "Good morning my little candy licker. I tried to wake you several times, but you were snoring so loud that you probably couldn't hear me. Lol Anyway, thank you for a great time last night. You are amazing in bed. I can't remember the last time I came so much. As much as I wanted to get a good morning round in before I left, I had to leave out for work. Hopefully you enjoyed yourself as much as I did so that I can get another shot at that good morning round. Maybe next time I can cook for you at my place. Have a good day!" Melanie's text lit up Ebonee's face like a department store's Christmas tree. Before she could put the phone down it began to ring. Normally she would ignore phone calls from numbers that she didn't recognize but after the night she had, there wasn't a telemarketer alive that could ruin her day.

Zaddy Issues

"Helloooo" she answered. A female voice on the other end responded, "Hi is this Ebonee?" The caller didn't sound like a telemarketer. She sounded like she was making a personal call rather than a business call. "It depends. Who is this?" Ebonee snapped. There was a snicker from the caller. Then she said "This is Monica. We met a few weeks ago at Malcolm's. I'm the one that cooked breakfast f or you two. Remember?" Ebonee let out a deep sigh and said "I remember you. But what I don't remember is giving you my phone number. You know this shit is creepy right? Wait…did Malcolm put you up to this?" Again, there was more snickering. "Not at all. Malcolm doesn't even know that I'm calling" Monica responded. "Then why are you calling me? And again, how did you get my number?" Ebonee asked growing more frustrated. "Well, I have access to everything of his. And like he said, I pretty much help him with everything. That's why I'm calling you. If you would be kind enough to meet me today for lunch, I'd like to have a woman to woman, face to face talk with you." Ebonee paused for a moment then asked, "And why would I meet with you?" Monica cleverly responded "Because he really cares for you. And I know you care for him as well." Ebonee smacked her lips then laughed and said, "You think?" Monica giggled and said "Yeah, I think. Otherwise, you would have hung up in my face long ago. Besides, Malcolm is a wonderful person. It's easy to care for someone like that. Anyway, I'll be at Miguel's on..." Before Monica could finish Ebonee blurted out "I know where Miguel's is." Monica responded "Good, hopefully I'll see you there. I'll be there right at twelve noon. They have great food as I'm sure you're aware."

When they got off of the phone Ebonee decided to check the messages from Malcolm. The majority were requesting a chance to explain or for a return call. After five or six messages she stopped reading and left the remaining texts unread. She got dressed for the day and reached out to the girls for something to get into. Gina and Nicole were both busy spending time doing things with their families and unable to get away. The day was getting away and Ebonee was left with nothing to do. Finally, she decided to take Monica up on her offer. Miguel's had great food and if she was going to go then she was going to make Monica pay for the meal. That way she'd at least get something out of it other than a bunch of useless begging on Malcolm's behalf. When Ebonee arrived at Miguel's she immediately spotted Monica sitting alone at a table. Monica looked up from her menu then spotted Ebonee also. She motioned for Ebonee to come join her. Ebonee made her way through the crowded

Zaddy Issues

restaurant to take her seat. "Thank you for coming. I'm glad you decided to join me" Monica expressed as she flagged down her waitress. "Like you said, they have great food here. So, I'm here now. You wanted to talk. So talk! What's so important that you couldn't say it over the phone that I had to come all the way here to hear?" The waitress walked up and handed Ebonee a menu before Monica could respond. "Good afternoon. My name is Michelle. I will be your waitress this afternoon. Would you care for something to drink while you decide on what to order?" the waitress asked. "I'm going to have another mimosa while we decide. Would you care for one?" Monica asked. Ebonee grinned and nodded. "I'll go get your drinks while you ladies decide on what you would like to order" the waitress informed them before walking off.

Monica took a sip of her mimosa and said, "I don't know if you've ever had a mimosa from here, but they are really good." Ebonee was getting aggravated with Monica and growled "Cut the shit. If you have something to tell me then spit it out already." Monica calmly stared at Ebonee equally aggravated and said "Me cut the shit? No, you cut the shit. He cares about you, and you care about him too. Now Michelle is about to bring us our drinks and take our orders. When she leaves, I will tell you everything you need to

Zaddy Issues

know. But you are NOT going to keep talking to me like I'm some DOG!" Monica realized she was getting out of character and had to gather her composure just as Michelle was walking up with their drinks. "Here you are. Are you ladies ready to order now?" Michelle asked looking back and forth at the two. Monica looked up at Michelle and said with a smile "I'll take the fish and chips with a side salad please. And I have a feeling you can bring us a pitcher of mimosa, so you don't have to keep running back and forth. What do you think Ebonee? Are you going to be here long enough to finish a pitcher with me?" As bad as Ebonee wanted to get up and walk away she didn't want to leave without hearing what Monica had to say. Ebonee dug up a smile and said "Absolutely. From the sounds of things, I just might need it. And I'll have the soup and sandwich of the day." Michelle grabbed the menus then smiled and said "Two excellent choices. I'll bring your pitcher out with your food. Neither meal takes long to prepare." Michelle walked off and Ebonee took a deep breath. She said "Look, I apologize. But this is a lot. I don't know what's going on. I'm just trying to get some answers." Monica smiled and said "Trust me I understand. Malcolm is an extraordinary man. And that crazy ass Ashley is under the impression that every woman is after his money. I get it but that's just not the case. I mean sure it's always a possibility that he may encounter a thirsty gold digger every now and then. But that comes with the territory. And Malcolm's pretty good at recognizing people that want to take advantage or exploit him for money. He doesn't need Ashley to be a guardian. He was making and holding onto his money long before any of us were even born. But she can't seem to get that through all of that overpriced weave on her head." Ebonee giggled as she thought back on her encounter with Ashley and the excessive amount of hair Ashley was sporting. She began to feel more relaxed knowing that she and Monica shared a common sentiment towards Ashley. Their waitress Michelle walked up with their food and mimosa pitcher then set everything on their table. "Can I get you ladies anything else?" Michelle politely asked. "You've brought everything that we need. Thanks!" Monica responded.

While they ate Monica explained how Malcolm was such an inspiration to all of the women that Ashley accused of being in his so-called stable of women. She told Ebonee about stories of how Malcolm helped provide shelter and employment for tons of black women that were not as fortunate enough to have a caring wealthy family member as Ashley, let alone have a father at all in a lot of the cases. Ebonee expected Monica to speak highly favorable of

Zaddy Issues

Malcolm, but she was not expecting to hear that. Monica was finishing of the last of her meal when Ebonee asked "So he's helped all of these women just to be nice? I hope you don't expect me to believe that he didn't sleep with any of them. I'm not stupid. He even told me himself that he didn't want to be in a monogamous relationship." Monica laughed then carefully dabbed at her mouth with her napkin and said, "I never said he didn't sleep with any." Ebonee rolled her eyes then sat back in her seat with her arms fold and started to look off to pout. Monica gasped loudly then leaned forward in her seat with both hands gripping the table and said, "Now I know you didn't think a fine, rich, single black man isn't going to sling all off the pipe that he wants and when he wants." Ebonee's facial expression was loudly saying "I'm not trying to hear any of this." Monica sat back in her seat then topped off her mimosa and told Ebonee "It's time for you to grow up. You're too old to sitting around with your lip poked out…especially over some dick. Yeah…you need to grow up." Monica had yet again become aggravated with Ebonee. Monica again calmed herself down and politely asked Ebonee "Have you ever heard of The Mahogany Vineyard?" Ebonee's eyes perked up and she answered "Yes of course. I was just there a few weeks ago. Why?" Monica smirked and said "Well Malcolm is the heir to TMV. He uses that gigantic home to house and employ nearly fifty women that would be on the streets if it wasn't for him. Which is also why Ashley thinks that he's going to someday leave all of it to someone that stays there. It's the most asinine thing I've ever heard. The man just wants to help and he's in a position to make a difference. So, you and Ashley both need to just put your big girl panties on and grow the hell up."

Ebonee was stunned and at a loss for words. Slowly she turned back to Monica and nervously asked "What about you?" Monica laughed out and said "Oh baby I'll be forty in less than two months. I'm grown grown! I'm talking FULL GROWN!" Ebonee's eyes lowered, and she sheepishly reiterated "No. I mean…have you been with him too?" Monica kindly responded "Awww sweetie you don't have to worry about me. I'm happily married with two kids. I don't have the time for two dicks anymore. But its not important who he gets with or who he's been with in the past. You're who he wants now!" Slowly Ebonee looked up and said "It matters to me. If I'm not enough woman for him then there would be plenty to worry about." Monica reached across the table and gently placed her hand on top of Ebonee's hand then said "Look men like Malcolm travel all over the world constantly. It can be a lonely life sometimes. So, so what if he gets his dick sucked while he's away closing a business deal for a week or so? He lives a really stressful life. And to be honest he deserves to be allowed to relieve a little tension sometimes. And guess what? You're not going to always be available. But just because he finds pleasure in another woman's company doesn't mean that it will somehow devalue what the two of you share. He thinks that you're special and that's what matters the most. Sure, he has a salacious sexual appetite, but I've never heard him talk about or look at the others the way he does for you. Not even me. But you…he's crazy about you honey. And yes, I was his first after losing his wife but who knows, you could be his last. Just keep an open mind if you decide to give him another chance. And for the record…I think you should. You two look great together. Plus, you make him happier than he's been in years. Don't worry about who he's fucking as long as it's YOU that he's LOVING. And if you can get past that, he will change your entire world." Just as Monica was finishing her speech her phone buzzed. "Oh shit. That's my alarm for my nail appointment. I need to be getting out of here. Would you like to join me?" Monica said looking down at her phone. Ebonee was still trying to process all that she had just learned about the man she thought she knew. "No not this time. Maybe another time" Ebonee politely declined. Monica finished her drink then stood and said "Sure but

Zaddy Issues

remember what I said. I think you should give him another chance. You should go see him. He's staying at the vineyard while he recovers. He would love to see you. And I can tell that you still have feelings for him. Don't lie to yourself and miss out on something that could be great." Ebonee looked up and said, "Thank you…for everything." Monica smiled and said "No need to thank me. Just take care of the bill and call it even." Then she turned and walked away.

Chapter 23

Breaking News Across The City

Monica gave Ebonee plenty to think about throughout the day. That night she shared with the girls most of everything that Monica told her. She conveniently excluded the part about Malcolm being a polygamist. She felt that would be more than they could handle right then. It was bad enough that she was still trying to wrap her own mind around things. She didn't want to have to deal with the possible scrutiny from her friends. So, she kept that to herself. After speaking with the girls Ebonee fell into her nightly routine of catching the late-night news before going to bed. Ebonee turned on the television and a commercial was on. She ran to the kitchen to grab a bottle of water before the broadcast began. From the kitchen she could hear the intro music for the news station. "As we promised we have a recap on the police involved shooting and capture of the once unknown attacker that had been targeting African American women throughout the city for what the police thinks could have been for at least the past five to six months. Lisa James is on the scene where the shooting and capture occurred, leaving one officer in critical conditions while another officer and

Zaddy Issues

suspect both died on the scene. Tonight, we now have the names of both officers involved as well as the suspect. We turn it over to Lisa for more details" the news anchor reported. Ebonee rushed out of the kitchen to see what was being said. As she was walking back into the living room the reporter Lisa was on the screen with several police cars with their lights flashing set still in a parking lot behind her. There was yellow police tape stretched out across the lot while multiple police officers and others scurried around in the background. The scene then switched over to Lisa as she began reporting "Thank you Andy. I'm here in the parking lot of Maplewood Apartments located in the heart of the university area. As you can see behind me is the scene where everything happened. According to a Police Chief Adam Berry, earlier today around 1:00pm detectives were following up on tips received from an anonymous source on information regarding the recent attacks. Chief Berry says the Cyber Investigation Unit was working closely in conjunction with detectives to track down a predator. They say tips led them to the doorsteps of this man here on the screen we now know goes by the nickname T-Dawg. His real name is Trevor Wiseman police say" Ebonee's heart dropped to her stomach as she stared at the picture of Trevor on the screen.

Zaddy Issues

Just when Ebonee thought she had heard everything. Lisa continued with "Police say they received a tip from a friend of one of Wiseman's victims that led them to look into the victim's online dating profile on the widely used dating app Black And Single Charlotte. Police believe that Wiseman used the app to lure women in then gain their trust and eventually killed them. According to Chief Berry, Wiseman has a history of violence and abuse reaching as far back as his early teens. Wiseman has been imprisoned twice for multiple drug charges, money laundering, extortion and assault. Police are still investigating the case for a motive. A motive that wound up living Detective Warren Morales hospitalized in critical condition fighting for his life and his partner Melanie Mitchell whom which unfortunately lost hers. Officer Mitchell leaves behind a wife of five years. More information is expected to come at the conclusion of the investigation. For now, I am Lisa James reporting. Back to you Andy." Ebonee's eyes welled up as she stared motionlessly at the picture of both Melanie and Trevor plastered across the screen. She had never been so devastated in her life. There she sat full of mixed emotions towards two people that she thought she knew but actually never did. She never would have suspected Trevor to be a killer. The thoughts of how close she came to possibly being one of his victims had her stomach in knots. She thought back to their relationship and wondered if that's why he was so upset that she wasn't home when he popped up at her home unannounced. She credited being with Malcolm to possibly being the very reason she was still alive. But then the hurt for Melanie kicked in and she was torn up inside. Even though Melanie lied about being divorced she couldn't help for feeling sad for her wife. She felt like she was in a bad dream and wanted out. She turned off the television and sat silently crying like a baby. Her phone began to ring. She looked and saw that it was Gina calling. She knew what Gina was calling for, but she was in no mode to discuss the news about Trevor. There was no way she could talk to Gina right. She also ignored Nicole's call for the same reasons. It was all far too much to deal with. And to add them into the mix would have been a guaranteed overload. So instead, she went to bed and cried herself to sleep.

Chapter 24

Let Bygones Be Bygones

Ebonee spent the next few days to herself with limited contact with everyone. Gina and Nicole understood that she needed time and space. It was early one Sunday afternoon when Ebonee was finally beginning to come back around to her old self when she received a phone call from an unknown number while sitting at home going over restaurant expenses. She sent the caller straight to voicemail. Again, the phone rang for a second time and again she sent it to voicemail. Ebonee continued to bang away at keys on her laptop when moments later she received a text. She hesitated to answer but gave in to the urge. It was from the same unlisted phone number. She opened the text and it read "Ebonee this is Ashley. I really need to see you asap. This is about my father. I've tried calling you, but it kept going to voicemail. I'm at the house my father is having built. I'm sure you know how to find me. I hope that you come so we can be face to face when I say what I have to say. If you do come, pull around to the garage in the back. I will be here waiting for you for at least another hour." Ebonee jumped up like a scalded cat and slammed her laptop shut. "Oh, you

Zaddy Issues

picked the right day today bitch!" she mumbled to herself. She quickly changed into a pair of jeans, an old t-shirt and sneakers and was out of the house in record time. She couldn't believe Ashley would have the nerve to call and text her after the way she treated Ebonee the last time the saw each other. If it was a fight that she wanted, it was a fight she was going to get. Ebonee pulled up to the driveway and sped through the opened gate. She raced around to the back where Ashley was supposed to be. Ebonee parked directly behind Ashley's car to block her in to prevent her from getting away from the ass whooping she had coming. She jumped out yelling "I'm here! Let's talk! Ya ready? Huh? Let's go! Let's talk!" She started walking towards the opened garage and spotted Ashley trotting out of the house. Ashley was wearing a dress and high heels. She clearly wasn't dressed for a fist fight like Ebonee was. Ashley rushed up to Ebonee with a big smile on her face and her arms wide open for a hug. "Thank you so much for coming" Ashley said. Her approach confused Ebonee. "What in the hell is going on here?" Ebonee asked as Ashley gave her a big bear hug. "I'm so glad that you decided to come. I hope you didn't mind me calling. I know I was a real... how do I say..." Ashley started saying. Ebonee helped her and said "bitch. You were a real bitch, and I don't give a damn who your daddy is or what he has.

187 | P a g e

Zaddy Issues

You have no right going around talking to people like you're crazy just because you think someone wants his money." Ashley hung her head and said "I know. You're right. Do you mind coming inside so that we can get out of this wind and talk over a cup of coffee?" Ebonee rolled her eyes and said "No! But we can talk over a glass of wine. I know there's some here. I need something stronger than some coffee to calm me back down." Ashley smiled and said "Yes of course. Let's get inside. I'd rather have some wine too. I just didn't want to seem like an alcoholic."

They walked inside and Ebonee was surprised to find that the construction was completed with the exception of the kitchen area that she was supposed to design herself. "Oh woooow. It looks really nice in here now. The last time that I was here there was nothing but tools and unfinished walls" Ebonee explained. "Well, when daddy wants something done, he usually doesn't waste any time making it happen. Have a seat" Ashley said taking a seat at the kitchen table. Ebonee took a seat and said, "So how is Malcolm?" Ebonee asked. Ashley gave her half of a smile and said, "Well that's what I wanted to talk to you about." Ebonee instantly got concerned. "Oh no. Is there something wrong" she questioned. Ashley glanced away then back at Ebonee and said "Yes and no. You see I've come to realize that... How

Zaddy Issues

can I say this? I was wrong about you. As a matter of fact, I've been wrong about a lot. You have made my father the happiest that he's been since my mother passed. And I was wrong for the way I treated you. Hell, I was wrong for the way I've treated a lot of people lately. But most importantly I was definitely wrong for the way I've treated my father. I know now that he needs not someone like you. He needs YOU!" Ebonee rolled her eyes and said "He needs me huh? How is it that a man that can have any woman that he wants needs me. Besides, according to you he has a stable full of women. So, what makes me so special?" Ashley was embarrassed at hearing her own words coming from Ebonee. Ashley kind of grinned then said "Yeeeah about that! I was out of line. My father is free spirited, and I get it. He's definitely not your average everyday Joe. Women love him and he loves...women. BUUUUT...he's not IN love with them. My father has a big heart." Ebonee smirked and mumbled to herself "That ain't all he has that's big. Lord have mercy." Ashley quickly turned away covering her ears saying "Lalalalala... I don't want to hear about any of that." Ebonee smirked and said "I'm just saying. Your daddy is blessed!" Ashley frantically waved her hands around as though she was trying to fan away the words she heard. "Okay okaaaay! Please...stop. Listen, the point I'm trying to make is that I don't think that you should give up on him. These last few days have been miserable for him. He's even been talking about moving back to New York in a couple of days. I saw how happy you made him. And I've unfortunately seen how unhappy he is without you. Not to mention I've noticed how your face lights up when you talk about him. I honestly believe that if there's anyone that can make him truly happy that it's you. And me? I guess it's time that I put my big girl panties on and grow up." Ashley poured out.

Ebonee was genuinely moved by Ashley's sincerity, but she also had a light bulb moment in her head. She squinted and asked, "You've been talking to Monica, haven't you?" Ashley rolled her eyes then fell out laughing and said "Girl yes! How did you know?" Ebonee smiled and said, "Because she told me that I needed to put on my big girl panties too." They both burst out laughing together. "I can't stand that bitch" Ashley joked. "I know right?" Ebonee agreed laughing so hard that she was nearly in tears. Ashley stopped laughing then added "But she's a fly old bitch. I'll give her that. The bitch be dressing. I thought I be dressing. But her… that bitch keeps it fly to be damn near fifty." Ebonee stopped laughing also to vigorously nod in agreement with everything that Ashley was saying. She stopped nodding and

Zaddy Issues

asked "Wait what? She told me…" Ashley interrupted Ebonee and said "Girl who knows how old she really is? You know black doesn't crack. As far as we know she could be my father's age. But speaking of her, she and I have a spa appointment together that I need to be getting to myself. I'm trying to find out what her secrets are to staying so young looking." Ashley stood up and held her arms out to give Ebonee a goodbye hug. Ebonee stood and gave her a hug then said, "Well I guess I'll be seeing you soon so that we can get your wedding menu planned." Ashley giggled and said "Weeeeell not exactly. The wedding's been called off. Turns out my dad was right about my fiancé Darrius. He was a real piece of shit. I see why you dumped his ass!" Her words nearly gave Ebonee a stroke. "Don't worry. My dad doesn't know about you two. I found old pictures of you in his phone. Very nice and naughty ones too. I deleted them for you. I see why my dad is crazy about you. It wasn't your pictures that did it. It wasn't even the pictures from a woman he had listed as 'Family Dollar', nor the one listed as 'Targe' and not even the one listed as 'Home Depot'. It was the dick pics from some dude listed as 'Jack In The Box'. And we're not even going to talk about the ones from a guy listed as 'Burger KING'! Well actually Mr. Burger King had it going on. That brother was hung like curtains. I sent myself one of his pics. Wanna see?" Ebonee's jaw was dropped to the floor. Ebonee quickly turned her head with a look of disgust and said, "No I don't wanna see!" Then slowly she turned back around and said "Well...yeah. Let me see." Ashley didn't hesitate to dig into her purse to grab her phone. With a devilish grin she pulled the phone out to find the picture for Ebonee. She handed Ebonee the phone and said "and don't worry. Apparently, this whole dick fetish is new he just picked up. So, it was well after you. but look at what your boy likes now." Again, Ebonee's jaw dropped. "Oh my God! That man is almost as big Malc..." Ebonee started to say before she realized who she was talking to. She quickly handed the phone back to Ashley and said "I meant... I'm sorry." Ashley grabbed the phone and slammed it inside of her purse and said, "THANKS for ruining the picture for me." They both laughed and headed out together.

When they got outside Ashley asked "So are you going to see my father? Or are you going to just let him run away and hide himself in New York? There's not a lot of time. If you want him the way that I think you do, then don't wait or it might be too late. He's at the vineyard. Go to the main house. Someone will let you in and get him for you." Ebonee smiled and said "Maybe. But thanks for calling me out here for the talk. I needed this." She jumped in the car and headed home.

Zaddy Issues

On her ride back she thought about everything that she had been through within the past few weeks and was mind blown. She thought about how she had misjudged everyone. Even Darrius. She never would have thought that he would go both ways. Trevor turned out to be a serial killer. Melanie lied about her marital status for no reason. Malcolm was the only genuine person that she had dealt with ever. Her mind was racing just as fast as the engine in her car if not faster. She was less than five miles from home when she took the exit ramp to head to Mahogany Vineyards. She kept hearing Monica and Ashley in her head and realized that they were right about her feelings for Malcolm. She knew that there was some truth to what Ashley was saying as well. She knew that if she waited much longer that she may miss out on a once in a lifetime chance to find happiness. She pulled into the estate and sped down the long entrance way to the main house of the vineyard. She jumped out of her car and ran up the steps as fast as she could. She beat on the door like a crazed woman. She had made up her mind that she wanted Malcolm and she didn't care who answered the door. No one was going to get in her way. When the door finally crept open, she was prepared for anything except for looking eye to eye with Candace. Both of their eyes grew the size of golf balls. "What are you doing here?" Ebonee asked. Candace began to stutter "I...I...I..." Malcolm then walked up from behind her with his head down looking at two neckties. "Which one of these ties do you like most? And who's at the door?" Malcolm asked Candace without looking up until he heard Ebonee's voice. "It's me! And you should go with the blue one. Blue looks good on you." Ebonee despondently suggested. Malcolm looked up in shock. There the three of them stood speechless with Candace caught standing between Ebonee and the man she had just vowed not to let anyone do just that. Was this a part of putting her big girl panties on or should she beat the brakes off of Candace before turning around and leaving? Ebonee stood looking at the two wondering what to do next!

The End

Or maybe not...

www.ingramcontent.com/pod-product-compliance
Lightning Source LLC
Chambersburg PA
CBHW070513260626
47161CB00004B/1541